The Ball at Sceaux

Honore de Balzac

Contents

THE BALL AT SCEAUX

BY

Honore de Balzac

THE BALL AT SCEAUX
BY
HONORE DE BALZAC

Translated By Clara Bell
To Henri de Balzac, his brother Honore.

The Comte de Fontaine, head of one of the oldest families in Poitou, had served the Bourbon cause with intelligence and bravery during the war in La Vendee against the Republic. After having escaped all the dangers which threatened the royalist leaders during this stormy period of modern history, he was wont to say in jest, "I am one of the men who gave themselves to be killed on the steps of the throne." And the pleasantry had some truth in it, as spoken by a man left for dead at the bloody battle of Les Quatre Chemins. Though ruined by confiscation, the staunch Vendeen steadily refused the lucrative posts offered to him by the Emperor Napoleon. Immovable in his aristocratic faith, he had blindly obeyed its precepts when he thought it fitting to choose a companion for life. In spite of the blandishments of a rich but revolutionary parvenu, who valued the alliance at a high figure, he married Mademoiselle de Kergarouet, without a fortune, but belonging to one of the oldest families in Brittany.

When the second revolution burst on Monsieur de Fontaine he was encumbered with a large family. Though it was no part of the noble gentlemen's views to solicit favors, he yielded to his wife's wish, left his country estate, of which the income barely sufficed to maintain his children, and came to Paris. Saddened by seeing the greediness of his former comrades in the rush for places and dignities under the new Constitution, he was about to return to his property when he received a ministerial despatch, in which a well-known magnate announced to him his nomination as marechal de camp, or brigadier-general, under a rule which allowed the officers of the Catholic armies to count the twenty submerged years of Louis XVIII.'s reign as years of service. Some days later he further received, without any solicitation, ex officio, the crosses of the Legion of Honor and of Saint-Louis.

Shaken in his determination by these successive favors, due, as he supposed, to the monarch's remembrance, he was no longer satisfied with taking his family, as he had piously done every Sunday, to cry "Vive le Roi" in the hall of the Tuileries when the royal family passed through on their way to chapel; he craved the favor of a private audience. The audience, at once granted, was in no sense private. The royal drawing-room was full of old adherents, whose powdered heads, seen from above, suggested a carpet of snow. There the Count met some old friends, who received him somewhat coldly; but the princes he thought ADORABLE, an enthusiastic expression which escaped him when the most gracious of his masters, to whom the Count had supposed himself to be known only by name, came to shake hands with him, and spoke of him as the most thorough Vendeen of them all. Notwithstanding this ovation, none of these august persons thought of inquiring as to the sum of his losses, or of the money he had poured so generously into the chests of the Catholic regiments. He discovered, a little late, that he had made war at his own cost. Towards the end of the evening he thought he might venture on a witty allusion to the state of his affairs, similar, as it was, to that of many other gentlemen. His Majesty laughed heartily enough; any speech that bore the hall-mark of wit was certain to please him; but he nevertheless replied with one of those royal pleasantries whose sweetness is more formidable than the anger of a rebuke. One of the King's most intimate advisers took an opportunity of going up to the fortune-seeking Vendeen, and made him understand by a keen and polite hint that the time had not yet come for settling accounts with the sovereign; that there were bills of much longer standing than his on the books, and there, no doubt, they would remain, as part of the history of the Revolution. The Count prudently withdrew from the venerable group, which formed a respectful semi-circle before the august family; then, having extricated his sword, not without some difficulty, from among the lean legs which had got mixed up with it, he crossed the courtyard of the Tuileries and got into the hackney cab he had left on the quay. With the restive spirit, which is peculiar to the nobility of the old school, in whom still survives the memory of the League and the day of the Barricades (in 1588), he bewailed himself in his cab, loudly enough to compromise him, over the change that had come over the Court. "Formerly," he said to himself, "every one could speak freely to the King of his own little affairs; the nobles could ask him a favor, or for money, when it suited them, and nowadays one cannot recover the money advanced for his service without raising a scandal! By Heaven! the cross of Saint-Louis and the rank of brigadier-general will not make good the three hundred thousand livres I have spent, out and out, on the royal cause. I must speak to the King, face to face, in his own room."

This scene cooled Monsieur de Fontaine's ardor all the more effectually because his requests for an interview were never answered. And, indeed, he saw the upstarts of the Empire obtaining some of the offices reserved, under the old monarchy, for the highest families.

"All is lost!" he exclaimed one morning. "The King has certainly never been other than a revolutionary. But for Monsieur, who never derogates, and is some comfort to his faithful adherents, I do not know what hands the crown of France might not fall into if things are to go on like this. Their cursed constitutional system is the worst possible government, and can never suit France. Louis XVIII. and Monsieur Beugnot spoiled everything at Saint Ouen."

The Count, in despair, was preparing to retire to his estate, abandoning, with dignity, all claims to repayment. At this moment the events of the 20th March (1815) gave warning of a fresh storm, threatening to overwhelm the legitimate monarch and his defenders. Monsieur de Fontaine, like one of those generous souls who do not dismiss a servant in a torrent of rain; borrowed on his lands to follow the routed monarchy, without knowing whether this complicity in emigration would prove more propitious to him than his past devotion. But when he perceived that the companions of the King's exile were in higher favor than the brave men who had protested, sword in hand, against the establishment of the republic, he may perhaps have hoped to derive greater profit from this journey into a foreign land than from active and dangerous service in the heart of his own country. Nor was his courtier-like calculation one of these rash speculations which promise splendid results on paper, and are ruinous in effect. He was --to quote the wittiest and most successful of our diplomates--one of the faithful five hundred who shared the exile of the Court at Ghent, and one of the fifty thousand who returned with it. During the short banishment of royalty, Monsieur de Fontaine was so happy as to be employed by Louis XVIII., and found more than one opportunity of giving him proofs of great political honesty and sincere attachment. One evening, when the King had nothing better to do, he recalled Monsieur de Fontaine's witticism at the Tuileries. The old Vendeen did not let such a happy chance slip; he told his history with so much vivacity that a king, who never forgot anything, might remember it at a convenient season. The royal amateur of literature also observed the elegant style given to some notes which the discreet gentleman had been invited to recast. This little success stamped Monsieur de Fontaine on the King's memory as one of the loyal servants of the Crown.

At the second restoration the Count was one of those special envoys who were sent throughout the departments charged with absolute jurisdiction over the leaders of revolt; but he used his terrible powers with moderation. As soon as the temporary commission was ended, the High Provost found a seat in the Privy Council, became a deputy, spoke little, listened much, and changed his opinions very considerably. Certain circumstances, unknown to historians, brought him into such intimate relations with the Sovereign, that one day, as he came in, the shrewd monarch addressed him thus: "My friend Fontaine, I shall take care never to appoint you to be director-general, or minister. Neither you nor I, as employes, could keep our place on account of our opinions. Representative government has this advantage; it saves Us the trouble We used to have, of dismissing Our Secretaries of State. Our Council is a perfect inn-parlor, whither public opinion sometimes sends strange travelers; however, We can always find a place for Our faithful adherents."

This ironical speech was introductory to a rescript giving Monsieur de Fontaine an appointment as administrator in the office of Crown lands. As a consequence of the intelligent attention with which he listened to his royal Friend's sarcasms, his name always rose to His Majesty's lips when a commission was to be appointed of which the members were to receive a handsome salary. He had the good sense to hold his tongue about the favor with which he was honored, and knew how to entertain the monarch in those familiar chats in which Louis XVIII. delighted as much as in a well-written note, by his brilliant manner of repeating political anecdotes, and the political or parliamentary tittle-tattle --if the expression may pass--which at that time was rife. It is well known that he was immensely amused by every detail of his Gouvernementabilite--a word adopted by his facetious Majesty.

Thanks to the Comte de Fontaine's good sense, wit, and tact, every member of his numerous family, however young, ended, as he jestingly told his Sovereign, in attaching himself like a silkworm to the leaves of the Pay-List. Thus, by the King's intervention, his eldest son found a high and fixed position as a lawyer. The second, before the restoration a mere captain, was appointed to the command of a legion on the return from Ghent; then, thanks to the confusion of 1815, when the regulations were evaded, he passed into the bodyguard, returned to a line regiment, and found himself after the affair of the Trocadero a lieutenant-general with a commission in the Guards. The youngest, appointed sous-prefet, ere long became a legal official and director of a municipal board of the city of Paris, where he was safe from changes in Legislature. These bounties, bestowed without parade, and as secret as the favor enjoyed by the Count, fell unperceived. Though the father and his three sons each had sinecures enough to enjoy an income in salaries almost equal to that of a chief of department, their political good fortune excited no envy. In those early days of the constitutional system, few persons had very precise ideas of the peaceful domain of the civil service, where astute favorites managed to find an equivalent for the demolished abbeys. Monsieur le Comte de Fontaine, who till lately boasted that he had not read the Charter, and displayed such indignation at the greed of courtiers, had, before long, proved to his august master that he understood, as well as the King himself, the spirit and resources of the representative system. At the same time, notwithstanding the established careers open to his three sons, and the pecuniary advantages derived from four official appointments, Monsieur de Fontaine was the head of too large a family to be able to re-establish his fortune easily and rapidly.

His three sons were rich in prospects, in favor, and in talent; but he had three daughters, and was afraid of wearying the monarch's benevolence. It occurred to him to mention only one by one, these virgins eager to light their torches. The King had too much good taste to leave his work incomplete. The marriage of the eldest with a Receiver-General, Planat de Baudry, was arranged by one of those royal speeches which cost nothing and are worth millions. One evening, when the Sovereign was out of spirits, he smiled on hearing of the existence of another Demoiselle de Fontaine, for whom he found a husband in the person of a young magistrate, of inferior birth, no doubt, but wealthy, and whom he created Baron. When, the year after, the Vendeen spoke of Mademoiselle Emilie de Fontaine, the King replied in his thin sharp tones, "Amicus Plato sed magis amica Natio." Then, a few days later, he treated his "friend Fontaine" to a quatrain, harmless enough, which he styled an epigram, in which he made fun of these three daughters so skilfully introduced, under the form of a trinity. Nay, if report is to be believed, the monarch had found the point of the jest in the Unity of the three Divine Persons.

"If your Majesty would only condescend to turn the epigram into an epithalamium?" said the Count, trying to turn the sally to good account.

"Though I see the rhyme of it, I fail to see the reason," retorted the King, who did not relish any pleasantry, however mild, on the subject of his poetry.

From that day his intercourse with Monsieur de Fontaine showed less amenity. Kings enjoy contradicting more than people think. Like most youngest children, Emilie de Fontaine was a Benjamin spoilt by almost everybody. The King's coolness, therefore, caused the Count all the more regret, because no marriage was ever so difficult to arrange as that of this darling daughter. To understand all the obstacles we must make our way into the fine residence where the official was housed at the expense of the nation. Emilie had spent her childhood on the family estate, enjoying the abundance which suffices for the joys of early youth; her lightest wishes had been law to her sisters, her brothers, her mother, and even her father. All her relations doted on her. Having come to years of discretion just when her family was loaded with the favors of fortune, the enchantment of life continued. The luxury of Paris seemed to her just as natural as a wealth of flowers or fruit, or as the rural plenty which had been the joy of her first years. Just as in her childhood she had never been thwarted in the satisfaction of her playful desires, so now, at fourteen, she was still obeyed when she rushed into the whirl of fashion.

Thus, accustomed by degrees to the enjoyment of money, elegance of dress, of gilded drawing-rooms and fine carriages, became as necessary to her as the compliments of flattery, sincere or false, and the festivities and vanities of court life. Like most spoiled children, she tyrannized over those who loved her, and kept her blandishments for those who were indifferent. Her faults grew with her growth, and her parents were to gather the bitter fruits of this disastrous education. At the age of nineteen Emilie de Fontaine had not yet been pleased to make a choice from among the many young men whom her father's politics brought to his entertainments. Though so young, she asserted in society all the freedom of mind that a married woman can enjoy. Her beauty was so remarkable that, for her, to appear in a room was to be its queen; but, like sovereigns, she had no friends, though she was everywhere the object of attentions to which a finer nature than hers might perhaps have succumbed. Not a man, not even an old man, had it in him to contradict the opinions of a young girl whose lightest look could rekindle love in the coldest heart.

She had been educated with a care which her sisters had not enjoyed; painted pretty well, spoke Italian and English, and played the piano brilliantly; her voice, trained by the best masters, had a ring in it which made her singing irresistibly charming. Clever, and intimate with every branch of literature, she might have made folks believe that, as Mascarille says, people of quality come into the world knowing everything. She could argue fluently on Italian or Flemish painting, on the Middle Ages or the Renaissance; pronounced at haphazard on books new or old, and could expose the defects of a work with a cruelly graceful wit. The simplest thing she said was accepted by an admiring crowd as a fetfah of the Sultan by the Turks. She thus dazzled shallow persons; as to deeper minds, her natural tact enabled her to discern them, and for them she put forth so much fascination that, under cover of her charms, she escaped their scrutiny. This enchanting veneer covered a careless heart; the opinion--common to many young girls--that no one else dwelt in a sphere so lofty as to be able to understand the merits of her soul; and a pride based no less on her birth than on her beauty. In the absence of the overwhelming sentiment which, sooner or later, works havoc in a woman's heart, she spent her young ardor in an immoderate love of distinctions, and expressed the deepest contempt for persons of inferior birth. Supremely impertinent to all newly-created nobility, she made every effort to get her parents recognized as equals by the most illustrious families of the Saint-Germain quarter.

These sentiments had not escaped the observing eye of Monsieur de Fontaine, who more than once, when his two elder girls were married, had smarted under Emilie's sarcasm. Logical readers will be surprised to see the old Royalist bestowing his eldest daughter on a Receiver-General, possessed, indeed, of some old hereditary estates, but whose name was not preceded by the little word to which the throne owed so many partisans, and his second to a magistrate too lately Baronified to obscure the fact that his father had sold firewood. This noteworthy change in the ideas of a noble on the verge of his sixtieth year--an age when men rarely renounce their convictions--was due not merely to his unfortunate residence in the modern Babylon, where, sooner or later, country folks all get their corners rubbed down; the Comte de Fontaine's new political conscience was also a result of the King's advice and friendship. The philosophical prince had taken pleasure in converting the Vendeen to the ideas required by the advance of the nineteenth century, and the new aspect of the Monarchy. Louis XVIII. aimed at fusing parties as Napoleon had fused things and men. The legitimate King, who was not less clever perhaps than his rival, acted in a contrary direction. The last head of the House of Bourbon was just as eager to satisfy the third estate and the creations of the Empire, by curbing the clergy, as the first of the Napoleons had been to attract the grand old nobility, or to endow the Church. The Privy Councillor, being in the secret of these royal projects, had insensibly become one of the most prudent and influential leaders of that moderate party which most desired a fusion of opinion in the interests of the nation. He preached the expensive doctrines of constitutional government, and lent all his weight to encourage the political see-saw which enabled his master to rule France in the midst of storms. Perhaps Monsieur de Fontaine hoped that one of the sudden gusts of legislation, whose unexpected efforts then startled the oldest politicians, might carry him up to the rank of peer. One of his most rigid principles was to recognize no nobility in France but that of the peerage--the only families that might enjoy any privileges.

"A nobility bereft of privileges," he would say, "is a tool without a handle."

As far from Lafayette's party as he was from La Bourdonnaye's, he ardently engaged in the task of general reconciliation, which was to result in a new era and splendid fortunes for France. He strove to convince the families who frequented his drawing-room, or those whom he visited, how few favorable openings would henceforth be offered by a civil or military career. He urged mothers to give their boys a start in independent and industrial professions, explaining that military posts and high Government appointments must at last pertain, in a quite constitutional order, to the younger sons of members of the peerage. According to him, the people had conquered a sufficiently large share in practical government by its elective assembly, its appointments to law-offices, and those of the exchequer, which, said he, would always, as heretofore, be the natural right of the distinguished men of the third estate.

These new notions of the head of the Fontaines, and the prudent matches for his eldest girls to which they had led, met with strong resistance in the bosom of his family. The Comtesse de Fontaine remained faithful to the ancient beliefs which no woman could disown, who, through her mother, belonged to the Rohans. Although she had for a while opposed the happiness and fortune awaiting her two eldest girls, she yielded to those private considerations which husband and wife confide to each other when their heads are resting on the same pillow. Monsieur de Fontaine calmly pointed out to his wife, by exact arithmetic that their residence in Paris, the necessity for entertaining, the magnificence of the house which made up to them now for the privations so bravely shared in La Vendee, and the expenses of their sons, swallowed up the chief part of their income from salaries. They must therefore seize, as a boon from heaven, the opportunities which offered for settling their girls with such wealth. Would they not some day enjoy sixty--eighty--a hundred thousand francs a year? Such advantageous matches were not to be met with every day for girls without a portion. Again, it was time that they should begin to think of economizing, to add to the estate of Fontaine, and re-establish the old territorial fortune of the family. The Countess yielded to such cogent arguments, as every mother would have done in her place, though perhaps with a better grace; but she declared that Emilie, at any rate, should marry in such a way as to satisfy the pride she had unfortunately contributed to foster in the girl's young soul.

Thus events, which ought to have brought joy into the family, had introduced a small leaven of discord. The Receiver-General and the young lawyer were the objects of a ceremonious formality which the Countess and Emilie contrived to create. This etiquette soon found even ampler opportunity for the display of domestic tyranny; for Lieutenant-General de Fontaine married Mademoiselle Mongenod, the daughter of a rich banker; the President very sensibly found a wife in a young lady whose father, twice or thrice a millionaire, had traded in salt; and the third brother, faithful to his plebeian doctrines, married Mademoiselle Grossetete, the only daughter of the Receiver-General at Bourges. The three sisters-in-law and the two brothers-in-law found the high sphere of political bigwigs, and the drawing-rooms of the Faubourg Saint-Germain, so full of charm and of personal advantages, that they united in forming a little court round the overbearing Emilie. This treaty between interest and pride was not, however, so firmly cemented but that the young despot was, not unfrequently, the cause of revolts in her little realm. Scenes, which the highest circles would not have disowned, kept up a sarcastic temper among all the members of this powerful family; and this, without seriously diminishing the regard they professed in public, degenerated sometimes in private into sentiments far from charitable. Thus the Lieutenant-General's wife, having become a Baronne, thought herself quite as noble as a Kergarouet, and imagined that her good hundred thousand francs a year gave her the right to be as impertinent as her sister-in-law Emilie, whom she would sometimes wish to see happily married, as she announced that the daughter of some peer of France had married Monsieur So-and-So with no title to his name. The Vicomtesse de Fontaine amused herself by eclipsing Emilie in the taste and magnificence that were conspicuous in her dress, her furniture, and her carriages. The satirical spirit in which her brothers and sisters sometimes received the claims avowed by Mademoiselle de Fontaine roused her to wrath that a perfect hailstorm of sharp sayings could hardly mitigate. So when the head of the family felt a slight chill in the King's tacit and precarious friendship, he trembled all the more because, as a result of her sisters' defiant mockery, his favorite daughter had never looked so high.

In the midst of these circumstances, and at a moment when this petty domestic warfare had become serious, the monarch, whose favor Monsieur de Fontaine still hoped to regain, was attacked by the malady of which he was to die. The great political chief, who knew so well how to steer his bark in the midst of tempests, soon succumbed. Certain then of favors to come, the Comte de Fontaine made every effort to collect the elite of marrying men about his youngest daughter. Those who may have tried to solve the difficult problem of settling a haughty and capricious girl, will understand the trouble taken by the unlucky father. Such an affair, carried out to the liking of his beloved child, would worthily crown the career the Count had followed for these ten years at Paris. From the way in which his family claimed salaries under every department, it might be compared with the House of Austria, which, by intermarriage, threatens to pervade Europe. The old Vendeen was not to be discouraged in bringing forward suitors, so much had he his daughter's happiness at heart, but nothing could be more absurd than the way in which the impertinent young thing pronounced her verdicts and judged the merits of her adorers. It might have been supposed that, like a princess in the Arabian Nights, Emilie was rich enough and beautiful enough to choose from among all the princes in the world. Her objections were each more preposterous than the last: one had too thick knees and was bow-legged, another was short-sighted, this one's name was Durand, that one limped, and almost all were too fat. Livelier, more attractive, and gayer than ever after dismissing two or three suitors, she rushed into the festivities of the winter season, and to balls, where her keen eyes criticised the celebrities of the day, delighted in encouraging proposals which she invariably rejected.

Nature had bestowed on her all the advantages needed for playing the part of Celimene. Tall and slight, Emilie de Fontaine could assume a dignified or a frolicsome mien at her will. Her neck was rather long, allowing her to affect beautiful attitudes of scorn and impertinence. She had cultivated a large variety of those turns of the head and feminine gestures, which emphasize so cruelly or so happily a hint of a smile. Fine black hair, thick and strongly-arched eyebrows, lent her countenance an expression of pride, to which her coquettish instincts and her mirror had taught her to add terror by a stare, or gentleness by the softness of her gaze, by the set of the gracious curve of her lips, by the coldness or the sweetness of her smile. When Emilie meant to conquer a heart, her pure voice did not lack melody; but she could also give it a sort of curt clearness when she was minded to paralyze a partner's indiscreet tongue. Her colorless face and alabaster brow were like the limpid surface of a lake, which by turns is rippled by the impulse of a breeze and recovers its glad serenity when the air is still. More than one young man, a victim to her scorn, accused her of acting a part; but she justified herself by inspiring her detractors with the desire to please her, and then subjecting them to all her most contemptuous caprice. Among the young girls of fashion, not one knew better than she how to assume an air of reserve when a man of talent was introduced to her, or how to display the insulting politeness which treats an equal as an inferior, and to pour out her impertinence on all who tried to hold their heads on a level with hers. Wherever she went she seemed to be accepting homage rather than compliments, and even in a princess her airs and manner would have transformed the chair on which she sat into an imperial throne.

Monsieur de Fontaine discovered too late how utterly the education of the daughter he loved had been ruined by the tender devotion of the whole family. The admiration which the world is at first ready to bestow on a young girl, but for which, sooner or later, it takes its revenge, had added to Emilie's pride, and increased her self-confidence. Universal subservience had developed in her the selfishness natural to spoilt children, who, like kings, make a plaything of everything that comes to hand. As yet the graces of youth and the charms of talent hid these faults from every eye; faults all the more odious in a woman, since she can only please by self-sacrifice and unselfishness; but nothing escapes the eye of a good father, and Monsieur de Fontaine often tried to explain to his daughter the more important pages of the mysterious book of life. Vain effort! He had to lament his daughter's capricious indocility and ironical shrewdness too often to persevere in a task so difficult as that of correcting an ill-disposed nature. He contented himself with giving her from time to time some gentle and kind advice; but he had the sorrow of seeing his tenderest words slide from his daughter's heart as if it were of marble. A father's eyes are slow to be unsealed, and it needed more than one experience before the old Royalist perceived that his daughter's rare caresses were bestowed on him with an air of condescension. She was like young children, who seem to say to their mother, "Make haste to kiss me, that I may go to play." In short, Emilie vouchsafed to be fond of her parents. But often, by those sudden whims, which seem inexplicable in young girls, she kept aloof and scarcely ever appeared; she complained of having to share her father's and mother's heart with too many people; she was jealous of every one, even of her brothers and sisters. Then, after creating a desert about her, the strange girl accused all nature of her unreal solitude and her wilful griefs. Strong in the experience of her twenty years, she blamed fate, because, not knowing that the mainspring of happiness is in ourselves, she demanded it of the circumstances of life. She would have fled to the ends of the earth to escape a marriage such as those of her two sisters, and nevertheless her heart was full of horrible jealousy at seeing them married, rich, and happy. In short, she sometimes led her mother--who was as much a victim to her vagaries as Monsieur de Fontaine--to suspect that she had a touch of madness.

But such aberrations are quite inexplicable; nothing is commoner than this unconfessed pride developed in the heart of young girls belonging to families high in the social scale, and gifted by nature with great beauty. They are almost all convinced that their mothers, now forty or fifty years of age, can neither sympathize with their young souls, nor conceive of their imaginings. They fancy that most mothers, jealous of their girls, want to dress them in their own way with the premeditated purpose of eclipsing them or robbing them of admiration. Hence, often, secret tears and dumb revolt against supposed tyranny. In the midst of these woes, which become very real though built on an imaginary basis, they have also a mania for composing a scheme of life, while casting for themselves a brilliant horoscope; their magic consists in taking their dreams for reality; secretly, in their long meditations, they resolve to give their heart and hand to none but the man possessing this or the other qualification; and they paint in fancy a model to which, whether or no, the future lover must correspond. After some little experience of life, and the serious reflections that come with years, by dint of seeing the world and its prosaic round, by dint of observing unhappy examples, the brilliant hues of their ideal are extinguished. Then, one fine day, in the course of events, they are quite astonished to find themselves happy without the nuptial poetry of their day-dreams. It was on the strength of that poetry that Mademoiselle Emilie de Fontaine, in her slender wisdom, had drawn up a programme to which a suitor must conform to be excepted. Hence her disdain and sarcasm.

"Though young and of an ancient family, he must be a peer of France," said she to herself. "I could not bear not to see my coat-of-arms on the panels of my carriage among the folds of azure mantling, not to drive like the princes down the broad walk of the Champs-Elysees on the days of Longchamps in Holy Week. Besides, my father says that it will someday be the highest dignity in France. He must be a soldier --but I reserve the right of making him retire; and he must bear an Order, that the sentries may present arms to us."

And these rare qualifications would count for nothing if this creature of fancy had not the most amiable temper, a fine figure, intelligence, and, above all, if he were not slender. To be lean, a personal grace which is but fugitive, especially under a representative government, was an indispensable condition. Mademoiselle de Fontaine had an ideal standard which was to be the model. A young man who at the first glance did not fulfil the requisite conditions did not even get a second look.

"Good Heavens! see how fat he is!" was with her the utmost expression of contempt.

To hear her, people of respectable corpulence were incapable of sentiment, bad husbands, and unfit for civilized society. Though it is esteemed a beauty in the East, to be fat seemed to her a misfortune for a woman; but in a man it was a crime. These paradoxical views were amusing, thanks to a certain liveliness of rhetoric. The Count felt nevertheless that by-and-by his daughter's affections, of which the absurdity would be evident to some women who were not less clear-sighted than merciless, would inevitably become a subject of constant ridicule. He feared lest her eccentric notions should deviate into bad style. He trembled to think that the pitiless world might already be laughing at a young woman who remained so long on the stage without arriving at any conclusion of the drama she was playing. More than one actor in it, disgusted by a refusal, seemed to be waiting for the slightest turn of ill-luck to take his revenge. The indifferent, the lookers-on were beginning to weary of it; admiration is always exhausting to human beings. The old Vendeen knew better than any one that if there is an art in choosing the right moment for coming forward on the boards of the world, on those of the Court, in a drawing-room or on the stage, it is still more difficult to quit them in the nick of time. So during the first winter after the accession of Charles X., he redoubled his efforts, seconded by his three sons and his sons-in-law, to assemble in the rooms of his official residence the best matches which Paris and the various deputations from departments could offer. The splendor of his entertainments, the luxury of his dining-room, and his dinners, fragrant with truffles, rivaled the famous banquets by which the ministers of that time secured the vote of their parliamentary recruits.

The Honorable Deputy was consequently pointed at as a most influential corrupter of the legislative honesty of the illustrious Chamber that was dying as it would seem of indigestion. A whimsical result! his efforts to get his daughter married secured him a splendid popularity. He perhaps found some covert advantage in selling his truffles twice over. This accusation, started by certain mocking Liberals, who made up by their flow of words for their small following in the Chamber, was not a success. The Poitevin gentleman had always been so noble and so honorable, that he was not once the object of those epigrams which the malicious journalism of the day hurled at the three hundred votes of the centre, at the Ministers, the cooks, the Directors-General, the princely Amphitryons, and the official supporters of the Villele Ministry.

At the close of this campaign, during which Monsieur de Fontaine had on several occasions brought out all his forces, he believed that this time the procession of suitors would not be a mere dissolving view in his daughter's eyes; that it was time she should make up her mind. He felt a certain inward satisfaction at having well fulfilled his duty as a father. And having left no stone unturned, he hoped that, among so many hearts laid at Emilie's feet, there might be one to which her caprice might give a preference. Incapable of repeating such an effort, and tired, too, of his daughter's conduct, one morning, towards the end of Lent, when the business at the Chamber did not demand his vote, he determined to ask what her views were. While his valet was artistically decorating his bald yellow head with the delta of powder which, with the hanging "ailes de pigeon," completed his venerable style of hairdressing, Emilie's father, not without some secret misgivings, told his old servant to go and desire the haughty damsel to appear in the presence of the head of the family.

"Joseph," he added, when his hair was dressed, "take away that towel, draw back the curtains, put those chairs square, shake the rug, and lay it quite straight. Dust everything.--Now, air the room a little by opening the window."

The Count multiplied his orders, putting Joseph out of breath, and the old servant, understanding his master's intentions, aired and tidied the room, of course the least cared for of any in the house, and succeeded in giving a look of harmony to the files of bills, the letter-boxes, the books and furniture of this sanctum, where the interests of the royal demesnes were debated over. When Joseph had reduced this chaos to some sort of order, and brought to the front such things as might be most pleasing to the eye, as if it were a shop front, or such as by their color might give the effect of a kind of official poetry, he stood for a minute in the midst of the labyrinth of papers piled in some places even on the floor, admired his handiwork, jerked his head, and went.

The anxious sinecure-holder did not share his retainer's favorable opinion. Before seating himself in his deep chair, whose rounded back screened him from draughts, he looked round him doubtfully, examined his dressing-gown with a hostile expression, shook off a few grains of snuff, carefully wiped his nose, arranged the tongs and shovel, made the fire, pulled up the heels of his slippers, pulled out his little queue of hair which had lodged horizontally between the collar of his waistcoat and that of his dressing-gown restoring it to its perpendicular position; then he swept up the ashes of the hearth, which bore witness to a persistent catarrh. Finally, the old man did not settle himself till he had once more looked all over the room, hoping that nothing could give occasion to the saucy and impertinent remarks with which his daughter was apt to answer his good advice. On this occasion he was anxious not to compromise his dignity as a father. He daintily took a pinch of snuff, cleared his throat two or three times, as if he were about to demand a count out of the House; then he heard his daughter's light step, and she came in humming an air from Il Barbiere.

"Good-morning, papa. What do you want with me so early?" Having sung these words, as though they were the refrain of the melody, she kissed the Count, not with the familiar tenderness which makes a daughter's love so sweet a thing, but with the light carelessness of a mistress confident of pleasing, whatever she may do.

"My dear child," said Monsieur de Fontaine, gravely, "I sent for you to talk to you very seriously about your future prospects. You are at this moment under the necessity of making such a choice of a husband as may secure your durable happiness----"

"My good father," replied Emilie, assuming her most coaxing tone of voice to interrupt him, "it strikes me that the armistice on which we agreed as to my suitors is not yet expired."

"Emilie, we must to-day forbear from jesting on so important a matter. For some time past the efforts of those who most truly love you, my dear child, have been concentrated on the endeavor to settle you suitably; and you would be guilty of ingratitude in meeting with levity those proofs of kindness which I am not alone in lavishing on you."

As she heard these words, after flashing a mischievously inquisitive look at the furniture of her father's study, the young girl brought forward the armchair which looked as if it had been least used by petitioners, set it at the side of the fireplace so as to sit facing her father, and settled herself in so solemn an attitude that it was impossible not to read in it a mocking intention, crossing her arms over the dainty trimmings of a pelerine a la neige, and ruthlessly crushing its endless frills of white tulle. After a laughing side glance at her old father's troubled face, she broke silence.

"I never heard you say, my dear father, that the Government issued its instructions in its dressing-gown. However," and she smiled, "that does not matter; the mob are probably not particular. Now, what are your proposals for legislation, and your official introductions?"

"I shall not always be able to make them, headstrong girl!--Listen, Emilie. It is my intention no longer to compromise my reputation, which is part of my children's fortune, by recruiting the regiment of dancers which, spring after spring, you put to rout. You have already been the cause of many dangerous misunderstandings with certain families. I hope to make you perceive more truly the difficulties of your position and of ours. You are two-and-twenty, my dear child, and you ought to have been married nearly three years since. Your brothers and your two sisters are richly and happily provided for. But, my dear, the expenses occasioned by these marriages, and the style of housekeeping you require of your mother, have made such inroads on our income that I can hardly promise you a hundred thousand francs as a marriage portion. From this day forth I shall think only of providing for your mother, who must not be sacrificed to her children. Emilie, if I were to be taken from my family Madame de Fontaine could not be left at anybody's mercy, and ought to enjoy the affluence which I have given her too late as the reward of her devotion in my misfortunes. You see, my child, that the amount of your fortune bears no relation to your notions of grandeur. Even that would be such a sacrifice as I have not hitherto made for either of my children; but they have generously agreed not to expect in the future any compensation for the advantage thus given to a too favored child."

"In their position!" said Emilie, with an ironical toss of her head.

"My dear, do not so depreciate those who love you. Only the poor are generous as a rule; the rich have always excellent reasons for not handing over twenty thousand francs to a relation. Come, my child, do not pout, let us talk rationally.-- Among the young marrying men have you noticed Monsieur de Manerville?"

"Oh, he minces his words--he says Zules instead of Jules; he is always looking at his feet, because he thinks them small, and he gazes at himself in the glass! Besides, he is fair. I don't like fair men."

"Well, then, Monsieur de Beaudenord?"

"He is not noble! he is ill made and stout. He is dark, it is true. --If the two gentlemen could agree to combine their fortunes, and the first would give his name and his figure to the second, who should keep his dark hair, then--perhaps----"

"What can you say against Monsieur de Rastignac?"

"Madame de Nucingen has made a banker of him," she said with meaning.

"And our cousin, the Vicomte de Portenduere?"

"A mere boy, who dances badly; besides, he has no fortune. And, after all, papa, none of these people have titles. I want, at least, to be a countess like my mother."

"Have you seen no one, then, this winter----"

"No, papa."

"What then do you want?"

"The son of a peer of France.

"My dear girl, you are mad!" said Monsieur de Fontaine, rising.

But he suddenly lifted his eyes to heaven, and seemed to find a fresh fount of resignation in some religious thought; then, with a look of fatherly pity at his daughter, who herself was moved, he took her hand, pressed it, and said with deep feeling: "God is my witness, poor mistaken child, I have conscientiously discharged my duty to you as a father--conscientiously, do I say? Most lovingly, my Emilie. Yes, God knows! This winter I have brought before you more than one good man, whose character, whose habits, and whose temper were known to me, and all seemed worthy of you. My child, my task is done. From this day forth you are the arbiter of your fate, and I consider myself both happy and unhappy at finding myself relieved of the heaviest of paternal functions. I know not whether you will for any long time, now, hear a voice which, to you, has never been stern; but remember that conjugal happiness does not rest so much on brilliant qualities and ample fortune as on reciprocal esteem. This happiness is, in its nature, modest, and devoid of show. So now, my dear, my consent is given beforehand, whoever the son-in-law may be whom you introduce to me; but if you should be unhappy, remember you will have no right to accuse your father. I shall not refuse to take proper steps and help you, only your choice must be serious and final. I will never twice compromise the respect due to my white hairs."

The affection thus expressed by her father, the solemn tones of his urgent address, deeply touched Mademoiselle de Fontaine; but she concealed her emotion, seated herself on her father's knees--for he had dropped all tremulous into his chair again--caressed him fondly, and coaxed him so engagingly that the old man's brow cleared. As soon as Emilie thought that her father had got over his painful agitation, she said in a gentle voice: "I have to thank you for your graceful attention, my dear father. You have had your room set in order to receive your beloved daughter. You did not perhaps know that you would find her so foolish and so headstrong. But, papa, is it so difficult to get married to a peer of France? You declared that they were manufactured by dozens. At least, you will not refuse to advise me."

"No, my poor child, no;--and more than once I may have occasion to cry, 'Beware!' Remember that the making of peers is so recent a force in our government machinery that they have no great fortunes. Those who are rich look to becoming richer. The wealthiest member of our peerage has not half the income of the least rich lord in the English Upper Chamber. Thus all the French peers are on the lookout for great heiresses for their sons, wherever they may meet with them. The necessity in which they find themselves of marrying for money will certainly exist for at least two centuries.

"Pending such a fortunate accident as you long for--and this fastidiousness may cost you the best years of your life--your attractions might work a miracle, for men often marry for love in these days. When experience lurks behind so sweet a face as yours it may achieve wonders. In the first place, have you not the gift of recognizing virtue in the greater or smaller dimensions of a man's body? This is no small matter! To so wise a young person as you are, I need not enlarge on all the difficulties of the enterprise. I am sure that you would never attribute good sense to a stranger because he had a handsome face, or all the virtues because he had a fine figure. And I am quite of your mind in thinking that the sons of peers ought to have an air peculiar to themselves, and perfectly distinctive manners. Though nowadays no external sign stamps a man of rank, those young men will have, perhaps, to you the indefinable something that will reveal it. Then, again, you have your heart well in hand, like a good horseman who is sure his steed cannot bolt. Luck be with you, my dear!"

"You are making game of me, papa. Well, I assure you that I would rather die in Mademoiselle de Conde's convent than not be the wife of a peer of France."

She slipped out of her father's arms, and proud of being her own mistress, went off singing the air of Cara non dubitare, in the "Matrimonio Segreto."

As it happened, the family were that day keeping the anniversary of a family fete. At dessert Madame Planat, the Receiver-General's wife, spoke with some enthusiasm of a young American owning an immense fortune, who had fallen passionately in love with her sister, and made through her the most splendid proposals.

"A banker, I rather think," observed Emilie carelessly. "I do not like money dealers."

"But, Emilie," replied the Baron de Villaine, the husband of the Count's second daughter, "you do not like lawyers either; so that if you refuse men of wealth who have not titles, I do not quite see in what class you are to choose a husband."

"Especially, Emilie, with your standard of slimness," added the Lieutenant-General.

"I know what I want," replied the young lady.

"My sister wants a fine name, a fine young man, fine prospects, and a hundred thousand francs a year," said the Baronne de Fontaine. "Monsieur de Marsay, for instance."

"I know, my dear," retorted Emilie, "that I do not mean to make such a foolish marriage as some I have seen. Moreover, to put an end to these matrimonial discussions, I hereby declare that I shall look on anyone who talks to me of marriage as a foe to my peace of mind."

An uncle of Emilie's, a vice-admiral, whose fortune had just been increased by twenty thousand francs a year in consequence of the Act of Indemnity, and a man of seventy, feeling himself privileged to say hard things to his grand-niece, on whom he doted, in order to mollify the bitter tone of the discussion now exclaimed:

"Do not tease my poor little Emilie; don't you see she is waiting till the Duc de Bordeaux comes of age!"

The old man's pleasantry was received with general laughter.

"Take care I don't marry you, old fool!" replied the young girl, whose last words were happily drowned in the noise.

"My dear children," said Madame de Fontaine, to soften this saucy retort, "Emilie, like you, will take no advice but her mother's."

"Bless me! I shall take no advice but my own in a matter which concerns no one but myself," said Mademoiselle de Fontaine very distinctly.

At this all eyes were turned to the head of the family. Every one seemed anxious as to what he would do to assert his dignity. The venerable gentleman enjoyed much consideration, not only in the world; happier than many fathers, he was also appreciated by his family, all its members having a just esteem for the solid qualities by which he had been able to make their fortunes. Hence he was treated with the deep respect which is shown by English families, and some aristocratic houses on the continent, to the living representatives of an ancient pedigree. Deep silence had fallen; and the guests looked alternately from the spoilt girl's proud and sulky pout to the severe faces of Monsieur and Madame de Fontaine.

"I have made my daughter Emilie mistress of her own fate," was the reply spoken by the Count in a deep voice.

Relations and guests gazed at Mademoiselle de Fontaine with mingled curiosity and pity. The words seemed to declare that fatherly affection was weary of the contest with a character that the whole family knew to be incorrigible. The sons-in-law muttered, and the brothers glanced at their wives with mocking smiles. From that moment every one ceased to take any interest in the haughty girl's prospects of marriage. Her old uncle was the only person who, as an old sailor, ventured to stand on her tack, and take her broadsides, without ever troubling himself to return her fire.

When the fine weather was settled, and after the budget was voted, the whole family--a perfect example of the parliamentary families on the northern side of the Channel who have a footing in every government department, and ten votes in the House of Commons--flew away like a brood of young birds to the charming neighborhoods of Aulnay, Antony, and Chatenay. The wealthy Receiver-General had lately purchased in this part of the world a country-house for his wife, who remained in Paris only during the session. Though the fair Emilie despised the commonalty, her feeling was not carried so far as to scorn the advantages of a fortune acquired in a profession; so she accompanied her sister to the sumptuous villa, less out of affection for the members of her family who were visiting there, than because fashion has ordained that every woman who has any self-respect must leave

Paris in the summer. The green seclusion of Sceaux answered to perfection the requirements of good style and of the duties of an official position.

As it is extremely doubtful that the fame of the "Bal de Sceaux" should ever have extended beyond the borders of the Department of the Seine, it will be necessary to give some account of this weekly festivity, which at that time was important enough to threaten to become an institution. The environs of the little town of Sceaux enjoy a reputation due to the scenery, which is considered enchanting. Perhaps it is quite ordinary, and owes its fame only to the stupidity of the Paris townsfolk, who, emerging from the stony abyss in which they are buried, would find something to admire in the flats of La Beauce. However, as the poetic shades of Aulnay, the hillsides of Antony, and the valley of the Bieve are peopled with artists who have traveled far, by foreigners who are very hard to please, and by a great many pretty women not devoid of taste, it is to be supposed that the Parisians are right. But Sceaux possesses another attraction not less powerful to the Parisian. In the midst of a garden whence there are delightful views, stands a large rotunda open on all sides, with a light, spreading roof supported on elegant pillars. This rural baldachino shelters a dancing-floor. The most stuck-up landowners of the neighborhood rarely fail to make an excursion thither once or twice during the season, arriving at this rustic palace of Terpsichore either in dashing parties on horseback, or in the light and elegant carriages which powder the philosophical pedestrian with dust. The hope of meeting some women of fashion, and of being seen by them--and the hope, less often disappointed, of seeing young peasant girls, as wily as judges--crowds the ballroom at Sceaux with numerous swarms of lawyers' clerks, of the disciples of Aesculapius, and other youths whose complexions are kept pale and moist by the damp atmosphere of Paris back-shops. And a good many bourgeois marriages have had their beginning to the sound of the band occupying the centre of this circular ballroom. If that roof could speak, what love-stories could it not tell!

This interesting medley gave the Sceaux balls at that time a spice of more amusement than those of two or three places of the same kind near Paris; and it had incontestable advantages in its rotunda, and the beauty of its situation and its gardens. Emilie was the first to express a wish to play at being COMMON FOLK at this gleeful suburban entertainment, and promised herself immense pleasure in mingling with the crowd. Everybody wondered at her desire to wander through such a mob; but is there not a keen pleasure to grand people in an incognito? Mademoiselle de Fontaine amused herself with imagining all these town-bred figures; she fancied herself leaving the memory of a bewitching glance and smile stamped on more than one shopkeeper's heart, laughed beforehand at the damsels' airs, and sharpened her pencils for the scenes she proposed to sketch in her satirical album. Sunday could not come soon enough to satisfy her impatience.

The party from the Villa Planat set out on foot, so as not to betray the rank of the personages who were about to honor the ball with their presence. They dined early. And the month of May humored this aristocratic escapade by one of its finest evenings. Mademoiselle de Fontaine was quite surprised to find in the rotunda some quadrilles made up of persons who seemed to belong to the upper classes. Here and there, indeed, were some young men who look as though they must have saved for a month to shine for a day; and she perceived several couples whose too hearty glee suggested nothing conjugal; still, she could only glean instead of gathering a harvest. She was amused to see that pleasure in a cotton dress was so very like pleasure robed in satin, and that the girls of the middle class danced quite as well as ladies-- nay, sometimes better. Most of the women were simply and suitably dressed. Those who in this assembly represented the ruling power, that is to say, the country-folk, kept apart with wonderful politeness. In fact, Mademoiselle Emilie had to study the various elements that composed the mixture before she could find any subject for pleasantry. But she had not time to give herself up to malicious criticism, or opportunity for hearing many of the startling speeches which caricaturists so gladly pick up. The haughty young lady suddenly found a flower in this wide field--the metaphor is reasonable--whose splendor and coloring worked on her imagination with all the fascination of novelty. It often happens that we look at a dress, a hanging, a blank sheet of paper, with so little heed that we do not at first detect a stain or a bright spot which afterwards strikes the eye as though it had come there at the very instant when we see it; and by a sort of moral phenomenon somewhat resembling this, Mademoiselle de Fontaine discovered in a young man the external perfection of which she had so long dreamed.

Seated on one of the clumsy chairs which marked the boundary line of the circular floor, she had placed herself at the end of the row formed by the family party, so as to be able to stand up or push forward as her fancy moved her, treating the living pictures and groups in the hall as if she were in a picture gallery; impertinently turning her eye-glass on persons not two yards away, and making her remarks as though she were criticising or praising a study of a head, a painting of genre. Her eyes, after wandering over the vast moving picture, were suddenly caught by this figure, which seemed to have been placed on purpose in one corner of the canvas, and in the best light, like a person out of all proportion with the rest.

The stranger, alone and absorbed in thought, leaned lightly against one of the columns that supported the roof; his arms were folded, and he leaned slightly on one side as though he had placed himself there to have his portrait taken by a painter. His attitude, though full of elegance and dignity, was devoid of affectation. Nothing suggested that he had half turned his head, and bent it a little to the right like Alexander, or Lord Byron, and some other great men, for the sole purpose of attracting attention. His fixed gaze followed a girl who was dancing, and betrayed some strong feeling. His slender, easy frame recalled the noble proportions of the Apollo. Fine black hair curled naturally over a high forehead. At a glance Mademoiselle de Fontaine observed that his linen was fine, his gloves fresh, and evidently bought of a good maker, and his feet were small and well shod in boots of Irish kid. He had none of the vulgar trinkets displayed by the dandies of the National Guard or the Lovelaces of the counting-house. A black ribbon, to which an eye-glass was attached, hung over a waistcoat of the most fashionable cut. Never had the fastidious Emilie seen a man's eyes shaded by such long, curled lashes. Melancholy and passion were expressed in this face, and the complexion was of a manly olive hue. His mouth seemed ready to smile, unbending the corners of eloquent lips; but this, far from hinting at gaiety, revealed on the contrary a sort of pathetic grace. There was too much promise in that head, too much distinction in his whole person, to allow of one's saying, "What a handsome man!" or "What a fine man!" One wanted to know him. The most clear-sighted observer, on seeing this stranger, could not have helped taking him for a clever man attracted to this rural festivity by some powerful motive.

All these observations cost Emilie only a minute's attention, during which the privileged gentleman under her severe scrutiny became the object of her secret admiration. She did not say to herself, "He must be a peer of France!" but "Oh, if only he is noble, and he surely must be----" Without finishing her thought, she suddenly rose, and followed by her brother the General, she made her way towards the column, affecting to watch the merry quadrille; but by a stratagem of the eye, familiar to women, she lost not a gesture of the young man as she went towards him. The stranger politely moved to make way for the newcomers, and went to lean against another pillar. Emilie, as much nettled by his politeness as she might have been by an impertinence, began talking to her brother in a louder voice than good taste enjoined; she turned and tossed her head, gesticulated eagerly, and laughed for no particular reason, less to amuse her brother than to attract the attention of the imperturbable stranger. None of her little arts succeeded. Mademoiselle de Fontaine then followed the direction in which his eyes were fixed, and discovered the cause of his indifference.

In the midst of the quadrille, close in front of them, a pale girl was dancing; her face was like one of the divinities which Girodet has introduced into his immense composition of French Warriors received by Ossian. Emilie fancied that she recognized her as a distinguished milady who for some months had been living on a neighboring estate. Her partner was a lad of about fifteen, with red hands, and dressed in nankeen trousers, a blue coat, and white shoes, which showed that the damsel's love of dancing made her easy to please in the matter of partners. Her movements did not betray her apparent delicacy, but a faint flush already tinged her white cheeks, and her complexion was gaining color. Mademoiselle de Fontaine went nearer, to be able to examine the young lady at the moment when she returned to her place, while the side couples in their turn danced the figure. But the stranger went up to the pretty dancer, and leaning over, said in a gentle but commanding tone:

"Clara, my child, do not dance any more."

Clara made a little pouting face, bent her head, and finally smiled. When the dance was over, the young man wrapped her in a cashmere shawl with a lover's care, and seated her in a place sheltered from the wind. Very soon Mademoiselle de Fontaine, seeing them rise and walk round the place as if preparing to leave, found means to follow them under pretence of admiring the views from the garden. Her brother lent himself with malicious good-humor to the divagations of her rather eccentric wanderings. Emilie then saw the attractive couple get into an elegant tilbury, by which stood a mounted groom in livery. At the moment when, from his high seat, the young man was drawing the reins even, she caught a glance from his eye such as a man casts aimlessly at the crowd; and then she enjoyed the feeble satisfaction of seeing him turn his head to look at her. The young lady did the same. Was it from jealousy?

"I imagine you have now seen enough of the garden," said her brother. "We may go back to the dancing."

"I am ready," said she. "Do you think the girl can be a relation of Lady Dudley's?"

"Lady Dudley may have some male relation staying with her," said the Baron de Fontaine; "but a young girl!--No!"

Next day Mademoiselle de Fontaine expressed a wish to take a ride. Then she gradually accustomed her old uncle and her brothers to escorting her in very early rides, excellent, she declared for her health. She had a particular fancy for the environs of the hamlet where Lady Dudley was living. Notwithstanding her cavalry manoeuvres, she did not meet the stranger so soon as the eager search she pursued might have allowed her to hope. She went several times to the "Bal de Sceaux" without seeing the young Englishman who had dropped from the skies to pervade and beautify her dreams. Though nothing spurs on a young girl's infant passion so effectually as an obstacle, there was a time when Mademoiselle de Fontaine was on the point of giving up her strange and secret search, almost despairing of the success of an enterprise whose singularity may give some idea of the boldness of her temper. In point of fact, she might have wandered long about the village of Chatenay without meeting her Unknown. The fair Clara--since that was the name Emilie had overheard--was not English, and the stranger who escorted her did not dwell among the flowery and fragrant bowers of Chatenay.

One evening Emilie, out riding with her uncle, who, during the fine weather, had gained a fairly long truce from the gout, met Lady Dudley. The distinguished foreigner had with her in her open carriage Monsieur Vandenesse. Emilie recognized the handsome couple, and her suppositions were at once dissipated like a dream. Annoyed, as any woman must be whose expectations are frustrated, she touched up her horse so suddenly that her uncle had the greatest difficulty in following her, she had set off at such a pace.

"I am too old, it would seem, to understand these youthful spirits," said the old sailor to himself as he put his horse to a canter; "or perhaps young people are not what they used to be. But what ails my niece? Now she is walking at a foot-pace like a gendarme on patrol in the Paris streets. One might fancy she wanted to outflank that worthy man, who looks to me like an author dreaming over his poetry, for he has, I think, a notebook in his hand. My word, I am a great simpleton! Is not that the very young man we are in search of!"

At this idea the old admiral moderated his horse's pace so as to follow his niece without making any noise. He had played too many pranks in the years 1771 and soon after, a time of our history when gallantry was held in honor, not to guess at once that by the merest chance Emilie had met the Unknown of the Sceaux gardens. In spite of the film which age had drawn over his gray eyes, the Comte de Kergarouet could recognize the signs of extreme agitation in his niece, under the unmoved expression she tried to give to her features. The girl's piercing eyes were fixed in a sort of dull amazement on the stranger, who quietly walked on in front of her.

"Ay, that's it," thought the sailor. "She is following him as a pirate follows a merchantman. Then, when she has lost sight of him, she will be in despair at not knowing who it is she is in love with, and whether he is a marquis or a shopkeeper. Really these young heads need an old fogy like me always by their side . . ."

He unexpectedly spurred his horse in such a way as to make his niece's bolt, and rode so hastily between her and the young man on foot that he obliged him to fall back on to the grassy bank which rose from the roadside. Then, abruptly drawing up, the Count exclaimed:

"Couldn't you get out of the way?"

"I beg your pardon, monsieur. But I did not know that it lay with me to apologize to you because you almost rode me down."

"There, enough of that, my good fellow!" replied the sailor harshly, in a sneering tone that was nothing less than insulting. At the same time the Count raised his hunting-crop as if to strike his horse, and touched the young fellow's shoulder, saying, "A liberal citizen is a reasoner; every reasoner should be prudent."

The young man went up the bankside as he heard the sarcasm; then he crossed his arms, and said in an excited tone of voice, "I cannot suppose, monsieur, as I look at your white hairs, that you still amuse yourself by provoking duels----"

"White hairs!" cried the sailor, interrupting him. "You lie in your throat. They are only gray."

A quarrel thus begun had in a few seconds become so fierce that the younger man forgot the moderation he had tried to preserve. Just as the Comte de Kerga-rouet saw his niece coming back to them with every sign of the greatest uneasiness, he told his antagonist his name, bidding him keep silence before the young lady entrusted to his care. The stranger could not help smiling as he gave a visiting card to the old man, desiring him to observe that he was living at a country-house at Chevreuse; and, after pointing this out to him, he hurried away.

"You very nearly damaged that poor young counter-jumper, my dear," said the Count, advancing hastily to meet Emilie. "Do you not know how to hold your horse in?--And there you leave me to compromise my dignity in order to screen your folly; whereas if you had but stopped, one of your looks, or one of your pretty speeches--one of those you can make so prettily when you are not pert--would have set everything right, even if you had broken his arm."

"But, my dear uncle, it was your horse, not mine, that caused the accident. I really think you can no longer ride; you are not so good a horseman as you were last year.--But instead of talking nonsense----"

"Nonsense, by Gad! Is it nothing to be so impertinent to your uncle?"

"Ought we not to go on and inquire if the young man is hurt? He is limping, uncle, only look!"

"No, he is running; I rated him soundly."

"Oh, yes, uncle; I know you there!"

"Stop," said the Count, pulling Emilie's horse by the bridle, "I do not see the ne-cessity of making advances to some shopkeeper who is only too lucky to have been thrown down by a charming young lady, or the commander of La Belle-Poule."

"Why do you think he is anything so common, my dear uncle? He seems to me to have very fine manners."

"Every one has manners nowadays, my dear."

"No, uncle, not every one has the air and style which come of the habit of fre-quenting drawing-rooms, and I am ready to lay a bet with you that the young man is of noble birth."

"You had not long to study him."

"No, but it is not the first time I have seen him."

"Nor is it the first time you have looked for him," replied the admiral with a laugh.

Emilie colored. Her uncle amused himself for some time with her embarrassment; then he said: "Emilie, you know that I love you as my own child, precisely because you are the only member of the family who has the legitimate pride of high birth. Devil take it, child, who could have believed that sound principles would become so rare? Well, I will be your confidant. My dear child, I see that his young gentleman is not indifferent to you. Hush! All the family would laugh at us if we sailed under the wrong flag. You know what that means. We two will keep our secret, and I promise to bring him straight into the drawing-room."

"When, uncle?"

"To-morrow."

"But, my dear uncle, I am not committed to anything?"

"Nothing whatever, and you may bombard him, set fire to him, and leave him to founder like an old hulk if you choose. He won't be the first, I fancy?"

"You ARE kind, uncle!"

As soon as the Count got home he put on his glasses, quietly took the card out of his pocket, and read, "Maximilien Longueville, Rue de Sentier."

"Make yourself happy, my dear niece," he said to Emilie, "you may hook him with any easy conscience; he belongs to one of our historical families, and if he is not a peer of France, he infallibly will be."

"How do you know so much?"

"That is my secret."

"Then do you know his name?"

The old man bowed his gray head, which was not unlike a gnarled oak-stump, with a few leaves fluttering about it, withered by autumnal frosts; and his niece immediately began to try the ever-new power of her coquettish arts. Long familiar with the secret of cajoling the old man, she lavished on him the most childlike caresses, the tenderest names; she even went so far as to kiss him to induce him to divulge so important a secret. The old man, who spent his life in playing off these scenes on his niece, often paying for them with a present of jewelry, or by giving her his box at the opera, this time amused himself with her entreaties, and, above all, her caresses. But as he spun out this pleasure too long, Emilie grew angry, passed from coaxing to sarcasm and sulks; then, urged by curiosity, she recovered herself. The diplomatic admiral extracted a solemn promise from his niece that she would for the future be gentler, less noisy, and less wilful, that she would spend less, and, above all, tell him everything. The treaty being concluded, and signed by a kiss impressed on Emilie's white brow, he led her into a corner of the room, drew her on to his knee, held the card under the thumbs so as to hide it, and then uncovered the letters one by one, spelling the name of Longueville; but he firmly refused to show her anything more.

This incident added to the intensity of Mademoiselle de Fontaine's secret sentiment, and during chief part of the night she evolved the most brilliant pictures from the dreams with which she had fed her hopes. At last, thanks to chance, to which she had so often appealed, Emilie could now see something very unlike a chimera at the fountain-head of the imaginary wealth with which she gilded her married life. Ignorant, as all young girls are, of the perils of love and marriage, she was passionately captivated by the externals of marriage and love. Is not this as much as to say that her feeling had birth like all the feelings of extreme youth--sweet but cruel mistakes, which exert a fatal influence on the lives of young girls so inexperienced as to trust their own judgment to take care of their future happiness?

Next morning, before Emilie was awake, her uncle had hastened to Chevreuse. On recognizing, in the courtyard of an elegant little villa, the young man he had so determinedly insulted the day before, he went up to him with the pressing politeness of men of the old court.

"Why, my dear sir, who could have guessed that I should have a brush, at the age of seventy-three, with the son, or the grandson, of one of my best friends. I am a vice-admiral, monsieur; is not that as much as to say that I think no more of fighting a duel than of smoking a cigar? Why, in my time, no two young men could be intimate till they had seen the color of their blood! But 'sdeath, sir, last evening, sailor-like, I had taken a drop too much grog on board, and I ran you down. Shake hands; I would rather take a hundred rebuffs from a Longueville than cause his family the smallest regret."

However coldly the young man tried to behave to the Comte de Kergarouet, he could not resist the frank cordiality of his manner, and presently gave him his hand.

"You were going out riding," said the Count. "Do not let me detain you. But, unless you have other plans, I beg you will come to dinner to-day at the Villa Planat. My nephew, the Comte de Fontaine, is a man it is essential that you should know. Ah, ha! And I propose to make up to you for my clumsiness by introducing you to five of the prettiest women in Paris. So, so, young man, your brow is clearing! I am fond of young people, and I like to see them happy. Their happiness reminds me of the good times of my youth, when adventures were not lacking, any more than duels. We were gay dogs then! Nowadays you think and worry over everything, as though there had never been a fifteenth and a sixteenth century."

"But, monsieur, are we not in the right? The sixteenth century only gave religious liberty to Europe, and the nineteenth will give it political lib----"

"Oh, we will not talk politics. I am a perfect old woman--ultra you see. But I do not hinder young men from being revolutionary, so long as they leave the King at liberty to disperse their assemblies."

When they had gone a little way, and the Count and his companion were in the heart of the woods, the old sailor pointed out a slender young birch sapling, pulled up his horse, took out one of his pistols, and the bullet was lodged in the heart of the tree, fifteen paces away.

"You see, my dear fellow, that I am not afraid of a duel," he said with comical gravity, as he looked at Monsieur Longueville.

"Nor am I," replied the young man, promptly cocking his pistol; he aimed at the hole made by the Comte's bullet, and sent his own close to it.

"That is what I call a well-educated man," cried the admiral with enthusiasm.

During this ride with the youth, whom he already regarded as his nephew, he found endless opportunities of catechizing him on all the trifles of which a perfect knowledge constituted, according to his private code, an accomplished gentleman.

"Have you any debts?" he at last asked of his companion, after many other inquiries.

"No, monsieur."

"What, you pay for all you have?"

"Punctually; otherwise we should lose our credit, and every sort of respect."

"But at least you have more than one mistress? Ah, you blush, comrade! Well, manners have changed. All these notions of lawful order, Kantism, and liberty have spoilt the young men. You have no Guimard now, no Duthe, no creditors--and you know nothing of heraldry; why, my dear young friend, you are not fully fledged. The man who does not sow his wild oats in the spring sows them in the winter. If I have but eighty thousand francs a year at the age of seventy, it is because I ran through the capital at thirty. Oh! with my wife--in decency and honor. However, your imperfections will not interfere with my introducing you at the Pavillon Planat. Remember, you have promised to come, and I shall expect you."

"What an odd little old man!" said Longueville to himself. "He is so jolly and hale; but though he wishes to seem a good fellow, I will not trust him too far."

Next day, at about four o'clock, when the house party were dispersed in the drawing-rooms and billiard-room, a servant announced to the inhabitants of the Villa Planat, "Monsieur DE Longueville." On hearing the name of the old admiral's protege, every one, down to the player who was about to miss his stroke, rushed in, as much to study Mademoiselle de Fontaine's countenance as to judge of this phoenix of men, who had earned honorable mention to the detriment of so many rivals. A simple but elegant style of dress, an air of perfect ease, polite manners, a pleasant voice with a ring in it which found a response in the hearer's heart-strings, won the good-will of the family for Monsieur Longueville. He did not seem unaccustomed to the luxury of the Receiver-General's ostentatious mansion. Though his conversation was that of a man of the world, it was easy to discern that he had had a brilliant education, and that his knowledge was as thorough as it was extensive. He knew so well the right thing to say in a discussion on naval architecture, trivial, it is true, started by the old admiral, that one of the ladies remarked that he must have passed through the Ecole Polytechnique.

"And I think, madame," he replied, "that I may regard it as an honor to have got in."

In spite of urgent pressing, he refused politely but firmly to be kept to dinner, and put an end to the persistency of the ladies by saying that he was the Hippocrates of his young sister, whose delicate health required great care.

"Monsieur is perhaps a medical man?" asked one of Emilie's sisters-in-law with ironical meaning.

"Monsieur has left the Ecole Polytechnique," Mademoiselle de Fontaine kindly put in; her face had flushed with richer color, as she learned that the young lady of the ball was Monsieur Longueville's sister.

"But, my dear, he may be a doctor and yet have been to the Ecole Polytechnique--is it not so, monsieur?"

"There is nothing to prevent it, madame," replied the young man.

Every eye was on Emilie, who was gazing with uneasy curiosity at the fascinating stranger. She breathed more freely when he added, not without a smile, "I have not the honor of belonging to the medical profession; and I even gave up going into the Engineers in order to preserve my independence."

"And you did well," said the Count. "But how can you regard it as an honor to be a doctor?" added the Breton nobleman. "Ah, my young friend, such a man as you----"

"Monsieur le Comte, I respect every profession that has a useful purpose."

"Well, in that we agree. You respect those professions, I imagine, as a young man respects a dowager."

Monsieur Longueville made his visit neither too long nor too short. He left at the moment when he saw that he had pleased everybody, and that each one's curiosity about him had been roused.

"He is a cunning rascal!" said the Count, coming into the drawing-room after seeing him to the door.

Mademoiselle de Fontaine, who had been in the secret of this call, had dressed with some care to attract the young man's eye; but she had the little disappointment of finding that he did not bestow on her so much attention as she thought she deserved. The family were a good deal surprised at the silence into which she had retired. Emilie generally displayed all her arts for the benefit of newcomers, her witty prattle, and the inexhaustible eloquence of her eyes and attitudes. Whether it was that the young man's pleasing voice and attractive manners had charmed her, that she was seriously in love, and that this feeling had worked a change in her, her demeanor had lost all its affectations. Being simple and natural, she must, no doubt, have seemed more beautiful. Some of her sisters, and an old lady, a friend of the family, saw in this behavior a refinement of art. They supposed that Emilie, judging the man worthy of her, intended to delay revealing her merits, so as to dazzle him suddenly when she found that she pleased him. Every member of the family was curious to know what this capricious creature thought of the stranger; but when, during dinner, every one chose to endow Monsieur Longueville with some fresh quality which no one else had discovered, Mademoiselle de Fontaine sat for some time in silence. A sarcastic remark of her uncle's suddenly roused her from her apathy; she said, somewhat epigrammatically, that such heavenly perfection must cover some great defect, and that she would take good care how she judged so gifted a man at first sight.

"Those who please everybody, please nobody," she added; "and the worst of all faults is to have none."

Like all girls who are in love, Emilie cherished the hope of being able to hide her feelings at the bottom of her heart by putting the Argus-eyes that watched on the wrong tack; but by the end of a fortnight there was not a member of the large family party who was not in this little domestic secret. When Monsieur Longueville called for the third time, Emilie believed it was chiefly for her sake. This discovery gave her such intoxicating pleasure that she was startled as she reflected on it. There was something in it very painful to her pride. Accustomed as she was to be the centre of her world, she was obliged to recognize a force that attracted her outside herself; she tried to resist, but she could not chase from her heart the fascinating image of the young man.

Then came some anxiety. Two of Monsieur Longueville's qualities, very adverse to general curiosity, and especially to Mademoiselle de Fontaine's, were unexpected modesty and discretion. He never spoke of himself, of his pursuits, or of his family. The hints Emilie threw out in conversation, and the traps she laid to extract from the young fellow some facts concerning himself, he could evade with the adroitness of a diplomatist concealing a secret. If she talked of painting, he responded as a connoisseur; if she sat down to play, he showed without conceit that he was a very good pianist; one evening he delighted all the party by joining his delightful voice to Emilie's in one of Cimarosa's charming duets. But when they tried to find out whether he were a professional singer, he baffled them so pleasantly that he did not afford these women, practised as they were in the art of reading feelings, the least chance of discovering to what social sphere he belonged. However boldly the old uncle cast the boarding-hooks over the vessel, Longueville slipped away cleverly, so as to preserve the charm of mystery; and it was easy to him to remain the "handsome Stranger" at the Villa, because curiosity never overstepped the bounds of good breeding.

Emilie, distracted by this reserve, hoped to get more out of the sister than the brother, in the form of confidences. Aided by her uncle, who was as skilful in such manoeuvres as in handling a ship, she endeavored to bring upon the scene the hitherto unseen figure of Mademoiselle Clara Longueville. The family party at the Villa Planat soon expressed the greatest desire to make the acquaintance of so amiable a young lady, and to give her some amusement. An informal dance was proposed and accepted. The ladies did not despair of making a young girl of sixteen talk.

Notwithstanding the little clouds piled up by suspicion and created by curiosity, a light of joy shone in Emilie's soul, for she found life delicious when thus intimately connected with another than herself. She began to understand the relations of life. Whether it is that happiness makes us better, or that she was too fully occupied to torment other people, she became less caustic, more gentle, and indulgent. This change in her temper enchanted and amazed her family. Perhaps, at last, her selfishness was being transformed to love. It was a deep delight to her to look for the arrival of her bashful and unconfessed adorer. Though they had not uttered a word of passion, she knew that she was loved, and with what art did she not lead the stranger to unlock the stores of his information, which proved to be varied! She perceived that she, too, was being studied, and that made her endeavor to remedy the defects her education had encouraged. Was not this her first homage to love, and a bitter reproach to herself? She desired to please, and she was enchanting; she loved, and she was idolized. Her family, knowing that her pride would sufficiently protect her, gave her enough freedom to enjoy the little childish delights which give to first love its charm and its violence. More than once the young man and Mademoiselle de Fontaine walked, tete-a-tete, in the avenues of the garden, where nature was dressed like a woman going to a ball. More than once they had those conversations, aimless and meaningless, in which the emptiest phrases are those which cover the deepest feelings. They often admired together the setting sun and its gorgeous coloring. They gathered daisies to pull the petals off, and sang the most impassioned duets, using the notes set down by Pergolesi or Rossini as faithful interpreters to express their secrets.

The day of the dance came. Clara Longueville and her brother, whom the servants persisted in honoring with the noble DE, were the principle guests. For the first time in her life Mademoiselle de Fontaine felt pleasure in a young girl's triumph. She lavished on Clara in all sincerity the gracious petting and little attentions which women generally give each other only to excite the jealousy of men. Emilie, had, indeed, an object in view; she wanted to discover some secrets. But, being a girl, Mademoiselle Longueville showed even more mother-wit than her brother, for she did not even look as if she were hiding a secret, and kept the conversation to subjects unconnected with personal interests, while, at the same time, she gave it so much charm that Mademoiselle de Fontaine was almost envious, and called her "the Siren." Though Emilie had intended to make Clara talk, it was Clara, in fact, who questioned Emilie; she had meant to judge her, and she was judged by her; she was constantly provoked to find that she had betrayed her own character in some reply which Clara had extracted from her, while her modest and candid manner prohibited any suspicion of perfidy. There was a moment when Mademoiselle de Fontaine seemed sorry for an ill-judged sally against the commonalty to which Clara had led her.

"Mademoiselle," said the sweet child, "I have heard so much of you from Maximilien that I had the keenest desire to know you, out of affection for him; but is not a wish to know you a wish to love you?"

"My dear Clara, I feared I might have displeased you by speaking thus of people who are not of noble birth."

"Oh, be quite easy. That sort of discussion is pointless in these days. As for me, it does not affect me. I am beside the question."

Ambitious as the answer might seem, it filled Mademoiselle de Fontaine with the deepest joy; for, like all infatuated people, she explained it, as oracles are explained, in the sense that harmonized with her wishes; she began dancing again in higher spirits than ever, as she watched Longueville, whose figure and grace almost surpassed those of her imaginary ideal. She felt added satisfaction in believing him to be well born, her black eyes sparkled, and she danced with all the pleasure that comes of dancing in the presence of the being we love. The couple had never understood each other as well as at this moment; more than once they felt their finger tips thrill and tremble as they were married in the figures of the dance.

The early autumn had come to the handsome pair, in the midst of country festivities and pleasures; they had abandoned themselves softly to the tide of the sweetest sentiment in life, strengthening it by a thousand little incidents which any one can imagine; for love is in some respects always the same. They studied each other through it all, as much as lovers can.

"Well, well; a flirtation never turned so quickly into a love match," said the old uncle, who kept an eye on the two young people as a naturalist watches an insect in the microscope.

The speech alarmed Monsieur and Madame Fontaine. The old Vendeen had ceased to be so indifferent to his daughter's prospects as he had promised to be. He went to Paris to seek information, and found none. Uneasy at this mystery, and not yet knowing what might be the outcome of the inquiry which he had begged a Paris friend to institute with reference to the family of Longueville, he thought it his duty to warn his daughter to behave prudently. The fatherly admonition was received with mock submission spiced with irony.

"At least, my dear Emilie, if you love him, do not own it to him."

"My dear father, I certainly do love him; but I will await your permission before I tell him so."

"But remember, Emilie, you know nothing of his family or his pursuits."

"I may be ignorant, but I am content to be. But, father, you wished to see me married; you left me at liberty to make my choice; my choice is irrevocably made--what more is needful?"

"It is needful to ascertain, my dear, whether the man of your choice is the son of a peer of France," the venerable gentleman retorted sarcastically.

Emilie was silent for a moment. She presently raised her head, looked at her father, and said somewhat anxiously, "Are not the Longuevilles----?"

"They became extinct in the person of the old Duc de Rostein-Limbourg, who perished on the scaffold in 1793. He was the last representative of the last and younger branch."

"But, papa, there are some very good families descended from bastards. The history of France swarms with princes bearing the bar sinister on their shields."

"Your ideas are much changed," said the old man, with a smile.

The following day was the last that the Fontaine family were to spend at the Pavillon Planat. Emilie, greatly disturbed by her father's warning, awaited with extreme impatience the hour at which young Longueville was in the habit of coming, to wring some explanation from him. She went out after dinner, and walked alone across the shrubbery towards an arbor fit for lovers, where she knew that the eager youth would seek her; and as she hastened thither she considered of the best way to discover so important a matter without compromising herself--a rather difficult thing! Hitherto no direct avowal had sanctioned the feelings which bound her to this stranger. Like Maximilien, she had secretly enjoyed the sweetness of first love; but both were equally proud, and each feared to confess that love.

Maximilien Longueville, to whom Clara had communicated her not unfounded suspicions as to Emilie's character, was by turns carried away by the violence of a young man's passion, and held back by a wish to know and test the woman to whom he would be entrusting his happiness. His love had not hindered him from perceiving in Emilie the prejudices which marred her young nature; but before attempting to counteract them, he wished to be sure that she loved him, for he would no sooner risk the fate of his love than of his life. He had, therefore, persistently kept a silence to which his looks, his behavior, and his smallest actions gave the lie.

On her side, the self-respect natural to a young girl, augmented in Mademoiselle de Fontaine by the monstrous vanity founded on her birth and beauty, kept her from meeting the declaration half-way, which her growing passion sometimes urged her to invite. Thus the lovers had instinctively understood the situation without explaining to each other their secret motives. There are times in life when such vagueness pleases youthful minds. Just because each had postponed speaking too long, they seemed to be playing a cruel game of suspense. He was trying to discover whether he was beloved, by the effort any confession would cost his haughty mistress; she every minute hoped that he would break a too respectful silence.

Emilie, seated on a rustic bench, was reflecting on all that had happened in these three months full of enchantment. Her father's suspicions were the last that could appeal to her; she even disposed of them at once by two or three of those reflections natural to an inexperienced girl, which, to her, seemed conclusive. Above all, she was convinced that it was impossible that she should deceive herself. All the summer through she had not been able to detect in Maximilien a single gesture, or a single word, which could indicate a vulgar origin or vulgar occupations; nay more, his manner of discussing things revealed a man devoted to the highest interests of the nation. "Besides," she reflected, "an office clerk, a banker, or a merchant, would not be at leisure to spend a whole season in paying his addresses to me in the midst of woods and fields; wasting his time as freely as a nobleman who has life before him free of all care."

She had given herself up to meditations far more interesting to her than these preliminary thoughts, when a slight rustling in the leaves announced to her than Maximilien had been watching her for a minute, not probably without admiration.

"Do you know that it is very wrong to take a young girl thus unawares?" she asked him, smiling.

"Especially when they are busy with their secrets," replied Maximilien archly.

"Why should I not have my secrets? You certainly have yours."

"Then you really were thinking of your secrets?" he went on, laughing.

"No, I was thinking of yours. My own, I know."

"But perhaps my secrets are yours, and yours mine," cried the young man, softly seizing Mademoiselle de Fontaine's hand and drawing it through his arm.

After walking a few steps they found themselves under a clump of trees which the hues of the sinking sun wrapped in a haze of red and brown. This touch of natural magic lent a certain solemnity to the moment. The young man's free and eager action, and, above all, the throbbing of his surging heart, whose hurried beating spoke to Emilie's arm, stirred her to an emotion that was all the more disturbing because it was produced by the simplest and most innocent circumstances. The restraint under which the young girls of the upper class live gives incredible force to any explosion of feeling, and to meet an impassioned lover is one of the greatest dangers they can encounter. Never had Emilie and Maximilien allowed their eyes to say so much that they dared never speak. Carried a way by this intoxication, they easily forgot the petty stipulations of pride, and the cold hesitancies of suspicion. At first, indeed, they could only express themselves by a pressure of hands which interpreted their happy thoughts.

After slowing pacing a few steps in long silence, Mademoiselle de Fontaine spoke. "Monsieur, I have a question to ask you," she said trembling, and in an agitated voice. "But, remember, I beg, that it is in a manner compulsory on me, from the rather singular position I am in with regard to my family."

A pause, terrible to Emilie, followed these sentences, which she had almost stammered out. During the minute while it lasted, the girl, haughty as she was, dared not meet the flashing eye of the man she loved, for she was secretly conscious of the meanness of the next words she added: "Are you of noble birth?"

As soon as the words were spoken she wished herself at the bottom of a lake.

"Mademoiselle," Longueville gravely replied, and his face assumed a sort of stern dignity, "I promise to answer you truly as soon as you shall have answered in all sincerity a question I will put to you!" --He released her arm, and the girl suddenly felt alone in the world, as he said: "What is your object in questioning me as to my birth?"

She stood motionless, cold, and speechless.

"Mademoiselle," Maximilien went on, "let us go no further if we do not understand each other. I love you," he said, in a voice of deep emotion. "Well, then," he added, as he heard the joyful exclamation she could not suppress, "why ask me if I am of noble birth?"

"Could he speak so if he were not?" cried a voice within her, which Emilie believed came from the depths of her heart. She gracefully raised her head, seemed to find new life in the young man's gaze, and held out her hand as if to renew the alliance.

"You thought I cared very much for dignities?" said she with keen archness.

"I have no titles to offer my wife," he replied, in a half-sportive, half-serious tone. "But if I choose one of high rank, and among women whom a wealthy home has accustomed to the luxury and pleasures of a fine fortune, I know what such a choice requires of me. Love gives everything," he added lightly, "but only to lovers. Once married, they need something more than the vault of heaven and the carpet of a meadow."

"He is rich," she reflected. "As to titles, perhaps he only wants to try me. He has been told that I am mad about titles, and bent on marrying none but a peer's son. My priggish sisters have played me that trick."--"I assure you, monsieur," she said aloud, "that I have had very extravagant ideas about life and the world; but now," she added pointedly, looking at him in a perfectly distracting way, "I know where true riches are to be found for a wife."

"I must believe that you are speaking from the depths of your heart," he said,

with gentle gravity. "But this winter, my dear Emilie, in less than two months perhaps, I may be proud of what I shall have to offer you if you care for the pleasures
of wealth. This is the only secret I shall keep locked here," and he laid his hand on
his heart, "for on its success my happiness depends. I dare not say ours."

"Yes, yes, ours!"

Exchanging such sweet nothings, they slowly made their way back to rejoin
the company. Mademoiselle de Fontaine had never found her lover more amiable
or wittier: his light figure, his engaging manners, seemed to her more charming
than ever, since the conversation which had made her to some extent the possessor
of a heart worthy to be the envy of every woman. They sang an Italian duet with so
much expression that the audience applauded enthusiastically. Their adieux were in
a conventional tone, which concealed their happiness. In short, this day had been
to Emilie like a chain binding her more closely than ever to the Stranger's fate. The
strength and dignity he had displayed in the scene when they had confessed their
feelings had perhaps impressed Mademoiselle de Fontaine with the respect without
which there is no true love.

When she was left alone in the drawing-room with her father, the old man
went up to her affectionately, held her hands, and asked her whether she had gained
any light at to Monsieur Longueville's family and fortune.

"Yes, my dear father," she replied, "and I am happier than I could have hoped.
In short, Monsieur de Longueville is the only man I could ever marry."

"Very well, Emilie," said the Count, "then I know what remains for me to do."

"Do you know of any impediment?" she asked, in sincere alarm.

"My dear child, the young man is totally unknown to me; but unless he is not a
man of honor, so long as you love him, he is as dear to me as a son."

"Not a man of honor!" exclaimed Emilie. "As to that, I am quite easy. My uncle,
who introduced him to us, will answer for him. Say, my dear uncle, has he been a
filibuster, an outlaw, a pirate?"

"I knew I should find myself in this fix!" cried the old sailor, waking up. He
looked round the room, but his niece had vanished "like Saint-Elmo's fires," to use
his favorite expression.

"Well, uncle," Monsieur de Fontaine went on, "how could you hide from us all
you knew about this young man? You must have seen how anxious we have been.

Is Monsieur de Longueville a man of family?"

"I don't know him from Adam or Eve," said the Comte de Kergarouet. "Trusting to that crazy child's tact, I got him here by a method of my own. I know that the boy shoots with a pistol to admiration, hunts well, plays wonderfully at billiards, at chess, and at backgammon; he handles the foils, and rides a horse like the late Chevalier de Saint-Georges. He has a thorough knowledge of all our vintages. He is as good an arithmetician as Bareme, draws, dances, and sings well. The devil's in it! what more do you want? If that is not a perfect gentleman, find me a bourgeois who knows all this, or any man who lives more nobly than he does. Does he do anything, I ask you? Does he compromise his dignity by hanging about an office, bowing down before the upstarts you call Directors-General? He walks upright. He is a man.--However, I have just found in my waistcoat pocket the card he gave me when he fancied I wanted to cut his throat, poor innocent. Young men are very simple-minded nowadays! Here it is."

"Rue du Sentier, No. 5," said Monsieur de Fontaine, trying to recall among all the information he had received, something which might concern the stranger. "What the devil can it mean? Messrs. Palma, Werbrust & Co., wholesale dealers in muslins, calicoes, and printed cotton goods, live there.--Stay, I have it: Longueville the deputy has an interest in their house. Well, but so far as I know, Longueville has but one son of two-and-thirty, who is not at all like our man, and to whom he gave fifty thousand francs a year that he might marry a minister's daughter; he wants to be made a peer like the rest of 'em. --I never heard him mention this Maximilien. Has he a daughter? What is this girl Clara? Besides, it is open to any adventurer to call himself Longueville. But is not the house of Palma, Werbrust & Co. half ruined by some speculation in Mexico or the Indies? I will clear all this up."

"You speak a soliloquy as if you were on the stage, and seem to account me a cipher," said the old admiral suddenly. "Don't you know that if he is a gentleman, I have more than one bag in my hold that will stop any leak in his fortune?"

"As to that, if he is a son of Longueville's, he will want nothing; but," said Monsieur de Fontaine, shaking his head from side to side, "his father has not even washed off the stains of his origin. Before the Revolution he was an attorney, and the DE he has since assumed no more belongs to him than half of his fortune."

"Pooh! pooh! happy those whose fathers were hanged!" cried the admiral gaily.

Three or four days after this memorable day, on one of those fine mornings in the month of November, which show the boulevards cleaned by the sharp cold of an early frost, Mademoiselle de Fontaine, wrapped in a new style of fur cape, of which she wished to set the fashion, went out with two of her sisters-in-law, on whom she had been wont to discharge her most cutting remarks. The three women were tempted to the drive, less by their desire to try a very elegant carriage, and wear gowns which were to set the fashion for the winter, than by their wish to see a cape which a friend had observed in a handsome lace and linen shop at the corner of the Rue de la Paix. As soon as they were in the shop the Baronne de Fontaine pulled Emilie by the sleeve, and pointed out to her Maximilien Longueville seated behind the desk, and engaged in paying out the change for a gold piece to one of the workwomen with whom he seemed to be in consultation. The "handsome stranger" held in his hand a parcel of patterns, which left no doubt as to his honorable profession.

Emilie felt an icy shudder, though no one perceived it. Thanks to the good breeding of the best society, she completely concealed the rage in her heart, and answered her sister-in-law with the words, "I knew it," with a fulness of intonation and inimitable decision which the most famous actress of the time might have envied her. She went straight up to the desk. Longueville looked up, put the patterns in his pocket with distracting coolness, bowed to Mademoiselle de Fontaine, and came forward, looking at her keenly.

"Mademoiselle," he said to the shopgirl, who followed him, looking very much disturbed, "I will send to settle that account; my house deals in that way. But here," he whispered into her ear, as he gave her a thousand-franc note, "take this--it is between ourselves.--You will forgive me, I trust, mademoiselle," he added, turning to Emilie. "You will kindly excuse the tyranny of business matters."

"Indeed, monsieur, it seems to me that it is no concern of mine," replied Mademoiselle de Fontaine, looking at him with a bold expression of sarcastic indifference which might have made any one believe that she now saw him for the first time.

"Do you really mean it?" asked Maximilien in a broken voice.

Emilie turned her back upon him with amazing insolence. These words, spoken in an undertone, had escaped the ears of her two sisters-in-law. When, after buying the cape, the three ladies got into the carriage again, Emilie, seated with her back to the horses, could not resist one last comprehensive glance into the depths of the odious shop, where she saw Maximilien standing with his arms folded, in the attitude of a man superior to the disaster that has so suddenly fallen on him. Their eyes met and flashed implacable looks. Each hoped to inflict a cruel wound on the heart of a lover. In one instant they were as far apart as if one had been in China and the other in Greenland.

Does not the breath of vanity wither everything? Mademoiselle de Fontaine, a prey to the most violent struggle that can torture the heart of a young girl, reaped the richest harvest of anguish that prejudice and narrow-mindedness ever sowed in a human soul. Her face, but just now fresh and velvety, was streaked with yellow lines and red patches; the paleness of her cheeks seemed every now and then to turn green. Hoping to hide her despair from her sisters, she would laugh as she pointed out some ridiculous dress or passer-by; but her laughter was spasmodic. She was more deeply hurt by their unspoken compassion than by any satirical comments for which she might have revenged herself. She exhausted her wit in trying to engage them in a conversation, in which she tried to expend her fury in senseless paradoxes, heaping on all men engaged in trade the bitterest insults and witticisms in the worst taste.

On getting home, she had an attack of fever, which at first assumed a somewhat serious character. By the end of a month the care of her parents and of the physician restored her to her family.

Every one hoped that this lesson would be severe enough to subdue Emilie's nature; but she insensibly fell into her old habits and threw herself again into the world of fashion. She declared that there was no disgrace in making a mistake. If she, like her father, had a vote in the Chamber, she would move for an edict, she said, by which all merchants, and especially dealers in calico, should be branded on the forehead, like Berri sheep, down to the third generation. She wished that none but nobles should have the right to wear the antique French costume, which was so becoming to the courtiers of Louis XV. To hear her, it was a misfortune for France, perhaps, that there was no outward and visible difference between a merchant and a peer of France. And a hundred more such pleasantries, easy to imagine, were rapidly poured out when any accident brought up the subject.

But those who loved Emilie could see through all her banter a tinge of melancholy. It was clear that Maximilien Longueville still reigned over that inexorable heart. Sometimes she would be as gentle as she had been during the brief summer that had seen the birth of her love; sometimes, again, she was unendurable. Every one made excuses for her inequality of temper, which had its source in sufferings at once secret and known to all. The Comte de Kergarouet had some influence over her, thanks to his increased prodigality, a kind of consolation which rarely fails of its effect on a Parisian girl.

The first ball at which Mademoiselle de Fontaine appeared was at the Neapolitan ambassador's. As she took her place in the first quadrille she saw, a few yards away from her, Maximilien Longueville, who nodded slightly to her partner.

"Is that young man a friend of yours?" she asked, with a scornful air.

"Only my brother," he replied.

Emilie could not help starting. "Ah!" he continued, "and he is the noblest soul living----"

"Do you know my name?" asked Emilie, eagerly interrupting him.

"No, mademoiselle. It is a crime, I confess, not to remember a name which is on every lip--I ought to say in every heart. But I have a valid excuse. I have but just arrived from Germany. My ambassador, who is in Paris on leave, sent me here this evening to take care of his amiable wife, whom you may see yonder in that corner."

"A perfect tragic mask!" said Emilie, after looking at the ambassadress.

"And yet that is her ballroom face!" said the young man, laughing. "I shall have to dance with her! So I thought I might have some compensation." Mademoiselle de Fontaine courtesied. "I was very much surprised," the voluble young secretary went on, "to find my brother here. On arriving from Vienna I heard that the poor boy was ill in bed; and I counted on seeing him before coming to this ball; but good policy will always allow us to indulge family affection. The Padrona della case would not give me time to call on my poor Maximilien."

"Then, monsieur, your brother is not, like you, in diplomatic employment."

"No," said the attache, with a sigh, "the poor fellow sacrificed himself for me. He and my sister Clara have renounced their share of my father's fortune to make an eldest son of me. My father dreams of a peerage, like all who vote for the ministry. Indeed, it is promised him," he added in an undertone. "After saving up a little capital my brother joined a banking firm, and I hear he has just effected a speculation in Brazil which may make him a millionaire. You see me in the highest spirits at having been able, by my diplomatic connections, to contribute to his success. I am impatiently expecting a dispatch from the Brazilian Legation, which will help to lift the cloud from his brow. What do you think of him?"

"Well, your brother's face does not look to me like that of a man busied with money matters."

The young attache shot a scrutinizing glance at the apparently calm face of his partner.

"What!" he exclaimed, with a smile, "can young ladies read the thoughts of love behind the silent brow?"

"Your brother is in love, then?" she asked, betrayed into a movement of curiosity.

"Yes; my sister Clara, to whom he is as devoted as a mother, wrote to me that he had fallen in love this summer with a very pretty girl; but I have had no further news of the affair. Would you believe that the poor boy used to get up at five in the morning, and went off to settle his business that he might be back by four o'clock in the country where the lady was? In fact, he ruined a very nice thoroughbred that I had just given him. Forgive my chatter, mademoiselle; I have but just come home from Germany. For a year I have heard no decent French, I have been weaned from French faces, and satiated with Germans, to such a degree that, I believe, in my patriotic mania, I could talk to the chimeras on a French candlestick. And if I talk with a lack of reserve unbecoming in a diplomatist, the fault is yours, mademoiselle. Was it not you who pointed out my brother? When he is the theme I become inexhaustible. I should like to proclaim to all the world how good and generous he is. He gave up no less than a hundred thousand francs a year, the income from the Longueville property."

If Mademoiselle de Fontaine had the benefit of these important revelations, it was partly due to the skill with which she continued to question her confiding partner from the moment when she found that he was the brother of her scorned lover.

"And could you, without being grieved, see your brother selling muslin and calico?" asked Emilie, at the end of the third figure of the quadrille.

"How do you know that?" asked the attache. "Thank God, though I pour out a flood of words, I have already acquired the art of not telling more than I intend, like all the other diplomatic apprentices I know."

"You told me, I assure you."

Monsieur de Longueville looked at Mademoiselle de Fontaine with a surprise that was full of perspicacity. A suspicion flashed upon him. He glanced inquiringly from his brother to his partner, guessed everything, clasped his hands, fixed his eyes on the ceiling, and began to laugh, saying, "I am an idiot! You are the handsomest person here; my brother keeps stealing glances at you; he is dancing in spite of his illness, and you pretend not to see him. Make him happy," he added, as he led her back to her old uncle. "I shall not be jealous, but I shall always shiver a little at calling you my sister----"

The lovers, however, were to prove as inexorable to each other as they were to themselves. At about two in the morning, refreshments were served in an immense corridor, where, to leave persons of the same coterie free to meet each other, the tables were arranged as in a restaurant. By one of those accidents which always happen to lovers, Mademoiselle de Fontaine found herself at a table next to that at which the more important guests were seated. Maximilien was of the group. Emilie, who lent an attentive ear to her neighbors' conversation, overheard one of those dialogues into which a young woman so easily falls with a young man who has the grace and style of Maximilien Longueville. The lady talking to the young banker was a Neapolitan duchess, whose eyes shot lightning flashes, and whose skin had the sheen of satin. The intimate terms on which Longueville affected to be with her stung Mademoiselle de Fontaine all the more because she had just given her lover back twenty times as much tenderness as she had ever felt for him before.

"Yes, monsieur, in my country true love can make every kind of sacrifice," the Duchess was saying, in a simper.

"You have more passion than Frenchwomen," said Maximilien, whose burning gaze fell on Emilie. "They are all vanity."

"Monsieur," Emilie eagerly interposed, "is it not very wrong to calumniate your own country? Devotion is to be found in every nation."

"Do you imagine, mademoiselle," retorted the Italian, with a sardonic smile, "that a Parisian would be capable of following her lover all over the world?"

"Oh, madame, let us understand each other. She would follow him to a desert and live in a tent but not to sit in a shop."

A disdainful gesture completed her meaning. Thus, under the influence of her disastrous education, Emile for the second time killed her budding happiness, and destroyed its prospects of life. Maximilien's apparent indifference, and a woman's smile, had wrung from her one of those sarcasms whose treacherous zest always let her astray.

"Mademoiselle," said Longueville, in a low voice, under cover of the noise made by the ladies as they rose from the table, "no one will ever more ardently desire your happiness than I; permit me to assure you of this, as I am taking leave of you. I am starting for Italy in a few days."

"With a Duchess, no doubt?"

"No, but perhaps with a mortal blow."

"Is not that pure fancy?" asked Emilie, with an anxious glance.

"No," he replied. "There are wounds which never heal."

"You are not to go," said the girl, imperiously, and she smiled.

"I shall go," replied Maximilien, gravely.

"You will find me married on your return, I warn you," she said coquettishly.

"I hope so."

"Impertinent wretch!" she exclaimed. "How cruel a revenge!"

A fortnight later Maximilien set out with his sister Clara for the warm and poetic scenes of beautiful Italy, leaving Mademoiselle de Fontaine a prey to the most vehement regret. The young Secretary to the Embassy took up his brother's quarrel, and contrived to take signal vengeance on Emilie's disdain by making known the occasion of the lovers' separation. He repaid his fair partner with interest all the sarcasm with which she had formerly attacked Maximilien, and often made more than one Excellency smile by describing the fair foe of the counting-house, the amazon who preached a crusade against bankers, the young girl whose love had evaporated before a bale of muslin. The Comte de Fontaine was obliged to use his influence to procure an appointment to Russia for Auguste Longueville in order to protect his daughter from the ridicule heaped upon her by this dangerous young persecutor.

Not long after, the Ministry being compelled to raise a levy of peers to support the aristocratic party, trembling in the Upper Chamber under the lash of an illustrious writer, gave Monsieur Guiraudin de Longueville a peerage, with the title of Vicomte. Monsieur de Fontaine also obtained a peerage, the reward due as much to his fidelity in evil days as to his name, which claimed a place in the hereditary Chamber.

About this time Emilie, now of age, made, no doubt, some serious reflections on life, for her tone and manners changed perceptibly. Instead of amusing herself by saying spiteful things to her uncle, she lavished on him the most affectionate attentions; she brought him his stick with a persevering devotion that made the cynical smile, she gave him her arm, rode in his carriage, and accompanied him in all his drives; she even persuaded him that she liked the smell of tobacco, and read him his favorite paper La Quotidienne in the midst of clouds of smoke, which the malicious old sailor intentionally blew over her; she learned piquet to be a match for the old count; and this fantastic damsel even listened without impatience to his periodical narratives of the battles of the Belle-Poule, the manoeuvres of the Ville de Paris, M. de Suffren's first expedition, or the battle of Aboukir.

Though the old sailor had often said that he knew his longitude and latitude too well to allow himself to be captured by a young corvette, one fine morning Paris drawing-rooms heard the news of the marriage of Mademoiselle de Fontaine to the Comte de Kergarouet. The young Countess gave splendid entertainments to drown thought; but she, no doubt, found a void at the bottom of the whirlpool; luxury was ineffectual to disguise the emptiness and grief of her sorrowing soul; for the most part, in spite of the flashes of assumed gaiety, her beautiful face expressed unspoken melancholy. Emilie appeared, however, full of attentions and consideration for her old husband, who, on retiring to his rooms at night, to the sounds of a lively band, would often say, "I do not know myself. Was I to wait till the age of seventy-two to embark as pilot on board the Belle Emilie after twenty years of matrimonial galleys?"

The conduct of the young Countess was marked by such strictness that the most clear-sighted criticism had no fault to find with her. Lookers on chose to think that the vice-admiral had reserved the right of disposing of his fortune to keep his wife more tightly in hand; but this was a notion as insulting to the uncle as to the niece. Their conduct was indeed so delicately judicious that the men who were most interested in guessing the secrets of the couple could never decide whether the old Count regarded her as a wife or as a daughter. He was often heard to say that he had rescued his niece as a castaway after shipwreck; and that, for his part, he had never taken a mean advantage of hospitality when he had saved an enemy from the fury of the storm. Though the Countess aspired to reign in Paris and tried to keep pace with Mesdames the Duchesses de Maufrigneuse and du Chaulieu, the Marquises d'Espard and d'Aiglemont, the Comtesses Feraud, de Montcornet, and de Restaud, Madame de Camps, and Mademoiselle des Touches, she did not yield to the addresses of the young Vicomte de Portenduere, who made her his idol.

Two years after her marriage, in one of the old drawing-rooms in the Faubourg Saint-Germain, where she was admired for her character, worthy of the old school, Emilie heard the Vicomte de Longueville announced. In the corner of the room where she was sitting, playing piquet with the Bishop of Persepolis, her agitation was not observed; she turned her head and saw her former lover come in, in all the freshness of youth. His father's death, and then that of his brother, killed by the severe climate of Saint-Petersburg, had placed on Maximilien's head the hereditary plumes of the French peer's hat. His fortune matched his learning and his merits; only the day before his youthful and fervid eloquence had dazzled the Assembly. At this moment he stood before the Countess, free, and graced with all the advantages she had formerly required of her ideal. Every mother with a daughter to marry made amiable advances to a man gifted with the virtues which they attributed to him, as they admired his attractive person; but Emilie knew, better than any one, that the Vicomte de Longueville had the steadfast nature in which a wise woman sees a guarantee of happiness. She looked at the admiral who, to use his favorite expression, seemed likely to hold his course for a long time yet, and cursed the follies of her youth.

At this moment Monsieur de Persepolis said with Episcopal grace: "Fair lady, you have thrown away the king of hearts--I have won. But do not regret your money. I keep it for my little seminaries."

PARIS, December 1829.

The Codes Of Hammurabi And Moses
W. W. Davies

QTY

The discovery of the Hammurabi Code is one of the greatest achievements of archaeology, and is of paramount interest, not only to the student of the Bible, but also to all those interested in ancient history...

Religion   **ISBN:** *1-59462-338-4*

Pages:132
MSRP $12.95

The Theory of Moral Sentiments
Adam Smith

QTY

This work from 1749. contains original theories of conscience amd moral judgment and it is the foundation for systemof morals.

Philosophy **ISBN:** *1-59462-777-0*

Pages:536
MSRP $19.95

Jessica's First Prayer
Hesba Stretton

QTY

In a screened and secluded corner of one of the many railway-bridges which span the streets of London there could be seen a few years ago, from five o'clock every morning until half past eight, a tidily set-out coffee-stall, consisting of a trestle and board, upon which stood two large tin cans, with a small fire of charcoal burning under each so as to keep the coffee boiling during the early hours of the morning when the work-people were thronging into the city on their way to their daily toil...

Childrens   **ISBN:** *1-59462-373-2*

Pages:84
MSRP $9.95

My Life and Work
Henry Ford

QTY

Henry Ford revolutionized the world with his implementation of mass production for the Model T automobile. Gain valuable business insight into his life and work with his own auto-biography... "We have only started on our development of our country we have not as yet, with all our talk of wonderful progress, done more than scratch the surface. The progress has been wonderful enough but..."

Biographies/   **ISBN:** *1-59462-198-5*

Pages:300
MSRP $21.95

The Art of Cross-Examination
Francis Wellman

QTY

I presume it is the experience of every author, after his first book is published upon an important subject, to be almost overwhelmed with a wealth of ideas and illustrations which could readily have been included in his book, and which to his own mind, at least, seem to make a second edition inevitable. Such certainly was the case with me; and when the first edition had reached its sixth impression in five months, I rejoiced to learn that it seemed to my publishers that the book had met with a sufficiently favorable reception to justify a second and considerably enlarged edition. ..

Pages:412

Reference   **ISBN:** *1-59462-647-2*   *MSRP $19.95*

On the Duty of Civil Disobedience
Henry David Thoreau

QTY

Thoreau wrote his famous essay, On the Duty of Civil Disobedience, as a protest against an unjust but popular war and the immoral but popular institution of slave-owning. He did more than write—he declined to pay his taxes,   and was hauled off to gaol in consequence. Who can say how much this refusal of his hastened the end of the war and of slavery ?

Law   **ISBN:** *1-59462-747-9*   **Pages:48**

MSRP $7.45

Dream Psychology Psychoanalysis for Beginners
Sigmund Freud

QTY

Sigmund Freud, born Sigismund Schlomo Freud (May 6, 1856 - September 23, 1939), was a Jewish-Austrian neurologist and psychiatrist who co-founded the psychoanalytic school of psychology. Freud is best known for his theories of the unconscious mind, especially involving the mechanism of repression; his redefinition of sexual desire as mobile and directed towards a wide variety of objects; and his therapeutic techniques, especially his understanding of transference in the therapeutic relationship and the presumed value of dreams as sources of insight into unconscious desires.

Pages:196

Psychology   **ISBN:** *1-59462-905-6*   *MSRP $15.45*

The Miracle of Right Thought
Orison Swett Marden

QTY

Believe with all of your heart that you will do what you were made to do. When the mind has once formed the habit of holding cheerful, happy, prosperous pictures, it will not be easy to form the opposite habit. It does not matter how improbable or how far away this realization may see, or how dark the prospects may be, if we visualize them as best we can, as vividly as possible, hold tenaciously to them and vigorously struggle to attain them, they will gradually become actualized, realized in the life. But a desire, a longing without endeavor, a yearning abandoned or held indifferently will vanish without realization.

Pages:360

Self Help   **ISBN:** *1-59462-644-8*   *MSRP $25.45*

QTY

The Rosicrucian Cosmo-Conception Mystic Christianity *by Max Heindel*   ISBN: *1-59462-188-8* **$38.95**
The Rosicrucian Cosmo-conception is not dogmatic, neither does it appeal to any other authority than the reason of the student. It is: not controversial, but is: sent forth in the, hope that it may help to clear...   New Age/Religion Pages 646

Abandonment To Divine Providence *by Jean-Pierre de Caussade*   ISBN: *1-59462-228-0* **$25.95**
"The Rev. Jean Pierre de Caussade was one of the most remarkable spiritual writers of the Society of Jesus in France in the 18th Century. His death took place at Toulouse in 1751. His works have gone through many editions and have been republished...   Inspirational/Religion Pages 400

Mental Chemistry *by Charles Haanel*   ISBN: *1-59462-192-6* **$23.95**
Mental Chemistry allows the change of material conditions by combining and appropriately utilizing the power of the mind. Much like applied chemistry creates something new and unique out of careful combinations of chemicals the mastery of mental chemistry...   New Age Pages 354

The Letters of Robert Browning and Elizabeth Barret Barrett 1845-1846 vol II   ISBN: *1-59462-193-4* **$35.95**
by Robert Browning and Elizabeth Barrett   Biographies Pages 596

Gleanings In Genesis (volume I) *by Arthur W. Pink*   ISBN: *1-59462-130-6* **$27.45**
Appropriately has Genesis been termed "the seed plot of the Bible" for in it we have, in germ form, almost all of the great doctrines which are afterwards fully developed in the books of Scripture which follow...   Religion/Inspirational Pages 420

The Master Key *by L. W. de Laurence*   ISBN: *1-59462-001-6* **$30.95**
In no branch of human knowledge has there been a more lively increase of the spirit of research during the past few years than in the study of Psychology, Concentration and Mental Discipline. The requests for authentic lessons in Thought Control, Mental Discipline and...   New Age/Business Pages 422

The Lesser Key Of Solomon Goetia *by L. W. de Laurence*   ISBN: *1-59462-092-X* **$9.95**
This translation of the first book of the "Lernegton" which is now for the first time made accessible to students of Talismanic Magic was done, after careful collation and edition, from numerous Ancient Manuscripts in Hebrew, Latin, and French...   New Age/Occult Pages 92

Rubaiyat Of Omar Khayyam *by Edward Fitzgerald*   ISBN:*1-59462-332-5* **$13.95**
Edward Fitzgerald, whom the world has already learned, in spite of his own efforts to remain within the shadow of anonymity, to look upon as one of the rarest poets of the century, was born at Bredfield, in Suffolk, on the 31st of March, 1809. He was the third son of John Purcell...   Music Pages 172

Ancient Law *by Henry Maine*   ISBN: *1-59462-128-4* **$29.95**
The chief object of the following pages is to indicate some of the earliest ideas of mankind, as they are reflected in Ancient Law, and to point out the relation of those ideas to modern thought.   Religion/History Pages 452

Far-Away Stories *by William J. Locke*   ISBN: *1-59462-129-2* **$19.45**
"Good wine needs no bush, but a collection of mixed vintages does. And this book is just such a collection. Some of the stories I do not want to remain buried for ever in the museum files of dead magazine-numbers an author's not unpardonable vanity..."   Fiction Pages 272

Life of David Crockett *by David Crockett*   ISBN: *1-59462-250-7* **$27.45**
"Colonel David Crockett was one of the most remarkable men of the times in which he lived. Born in humble life, but gifted with a strong will, an indomitable courage, and unremitting perseverance...   Biographies/New Age Pages 424

Lip-Reading *by Edward Nitchie*   ISBN: *1-59462-206-X* **$25.95**
Edward B. Nitchie, founder of the New York School for the Hard of Hearing, now the Nitchie School of Lip-Reading, Inc, wrote "LIP-READING Principles and Practice". The development and perfecting of this meritorious work on lip-reading was an undertaking...   How-to Pages 400

A Handbook of Suggestive Therapeutics, Applied Hypnotism, Psychic Science   ISBN: *1-59462-214-0* **$24.95**
by Henry Munro   Health/New Age/Health/Self-help Pages 376

A Doll's House: and Two Other Plays *by Henrik Ibsen*   ISBN: *1-59462-112-8* **$19.95**
Henrik Ibsen created this classic when in revolutionary 1848 Rome. Introducing some striking concepts in playwriting for the realist genre, this play has been studied the world over.   Fiction/Classics/Plays 308

The Light of Asia *by sir Edwin Arnold*   ISBN: *1-59462-204-3* **$13.95**
In this poetic masterpiece, Edwin Arnold describes the life and teachings of Buddha. The man who was to become known as Buddha to the world was born as Prince Gautama of India but he rejected the worldly riches and abandoned the reigns of power when...   Religion/History/Biographies Pages 170

The Complete Works of Guy de Maupassant *by Guy de Maupassant*   ISBN: *1-59462-157-8* **$16.95**
"For days and days, nights and nights, I had dreamed of that first kiss which was to consecrate our engagement, and I knew not on what spot I should put my lips..."   Fiction/Classics Pages 240

The Art of Cross-Examination *by Francis L. Wellman*   ISBN: *1-59462-309-0* **$26.95**
Written by a renowned trial lawyer, Wellman imparts his experience and uses case studies to explain how to use psychology to extract desired information through questioning.   How-to/Science/Reference Pages 408

Answered or Unanswered? *by Louisa Vaughan*   ISBN: *1-59462-248-5* **$10.95**
Miracles of Faith in China   Religion Pages 112

The Edinburgh Lectures on Mental Science (1909) *by Thomas*   ISBN: *1-59462-008-3* **$11.95**
This book contains the substance of a course of lectures recently given by the writer in the Queen Street Hail, Edinburgh. Its purpose is to indicate the Natural Principles governing the relation between Mental Action and Material Conditions...   New Age/Psychology Pages 148

Ayesha *by H. Rider Haggard*   ISBN: *1-59462-301-5* **$24.95**
Verily and indeed it is the unexpected that happens! Probably if there was one person upon the earth from whom the Editor of this, and of a certain previous history, did not expect to hear again...   Classics Pages 380

Ayala's Angel *by Anthony Trollope*   ISBN: *1-59462-352-X* **$29.95**
The two girls were both pretty, but Lucy who was twenty-one who supposed to be simple and comparatively unattractive, whereas Ayala was credited, as her Bombwhat romantic name might show, with poetic charm and a taste for romance. Ayala when her father died was nineteen...   Fiction Pages 484

The American Commonwealth *by James Bryce*   ISBN: *1-59462-286-8* **$34.45**
An interpretation of American democratic political theory. It examines political mechanics and society from the perspective of Scotsman James Bryce   Politics Pages 572

Stories of the Pilgrims *by Margaret P. Pumphrey*   ISBN: *1-59462-116-0* **$17.95**
This book explores pilgrims religious oppression in England as well as their escape to Holland and eventual crossing to America on the Mayflower, and their early days in New England...   History Pages 268

QTY

The Fasting Cure *by Sinclair Upton*   ISBN: *1-59462-222-1* **$13.95**
In the Cosmopolitan Magazine for May, 1910, and in the Contemporary Review (London) for April, 1910, I published an article dealing with my experi-
ences in fasting. I have written a great many magazine articles, but never one which attracted so much attention... New Age/Self Help/Health Pages 164

Hebrew Astrology *by Sepharial*   ISBN: *1-59462-308-2* **$13.45**
In these days of advanced thinking it is a matter of common observation that we have left many of the old landmarks behind and that we are now pressing
forward to greater heights and to a wider horizon than that which represented the mind-content of our progenitors...   Astrology Pages 144

Thought Vibration or The Law of Attraction in the Thought World   ISBN: *1-59462-127-6* **$12.95**

by William Walker Atkinson   Psychology/Religion Pages 144

Optimism *by Helen Keller*   ISBN: *1-59462-108-X* **$15.95**
Helen Keller was blind, deaf, and mute since 19 months old, yet famously learned how to overcome these handicaps, communicate with the world, and
spread her lectures promoting optimism. An inspiring read for everyone...   Biographies/Inspirational Pages 84

Sara Crewe *by Frances Burnett*   ISBN: *1-59462-360-0* **$9.45**
In the first place, Miss Minchin lived in London. Her home was a large, dull, tall one, in a large, dull square, where all the houses were alike, and all the
sparrows were alike, and where all the door-knockers made the same heavy sound...   Childrens/Classic Pages 88

The Autobiography of Benjamin Franklin *by Benjamin Franklin*   ISBN: *1-59462-135-7* **$24.95**
The Autobiography of Benjamin Franklin has probably been more extensively read than any other American historical work, and no other book of its kind
has had such ups and downs of fortune. Franklin lived for many years in England, where he was agent...   Biographies/History Pages 332

Name	
Email	
Telephone	
Address	
City, State ZIP	

☐ **Credit Card**   ☐ **Check / Money Order**

Credit Card Number	
Expiration Date	
Signature	

Please Mail to: Book Jungle
PO Box 2226
Champaign, IL 61825
or Fax to: 630-214-0564

ORDERING INFORMATION

web: *www.bookjungle.com*
email: *sales@bookjungle.com*
fax: *630-214-0564*
mail: *Book Jungle PO Box 2226 Champaign, IL 61825*
or PayPal *to sales@bookjungle.com*

Please contact us for bulk discounts

DIRECT-ORDER TERMS

**20% Discount if You Order
Two or More Books**
Free Domestic Shipping!
Accepted: Master Card, Visa,
Discover, American Express